NINO

NINO

WRITTEN AND ILLUSTRATED

BY VALENTI ANGELO

NEW YORK · THE VIKING PRESS

NINO

WRITTEN AND ILLUSTRATED

BY VALENTI ANGELO

NEW YORK · THE VIKING PRESS

TO

VALDINE AND PETER

CONTENTS

CONTENTS

NINO

CHAPTER I

GREEN CORN AND CROWS

AMID the tall green stalks of corn small Nino lay asleep in a basket. The morning sun threw dappled shadows across his face, and dragon-flies poised above his head on whirring wings. Black crows cawed loudly in the air, and

[11]

butterflies swooped gently down to kiss his tiny brow. He was wrapped in a swaddling-cloth that bound his little body tightly. No hands were seen, and his tiny feet were hidden. For hours he would lie crying; sometimes he fell asleep. Tears dried on his rosy cheeks. He lay all day among the tall green corn. Sometimes he watched the deep blue sky above; sometimes he laughed when a lark sailed by.

Allinda, his mother, came to him. The crows flew away and the dragon-flies disappeared into the evening shadows. It was cool now in the half-light, and a quiet hung over the corn fields.

His mother lifted the basket gently. Nino opened his eyes and smiled. Allinda carried the basket in her strong arms and sang a lullaby as she walked homeward.

This was Nino's first summer. Winter passed, and by the time summer came again, Nino had learned to crawl, and at last to walk, holding on to the chairs and table. The long swaddling-cloth was laid away now, and he was free to stand and to stagger about on his two sturdy legs. His mother still carried him to the fields every day, but he had grown too big and heavy for the basket. He sat on a blanket on the ground and watched her while she worked. Allinda gave him a little stick, and he dug with it in the warm brown earth, and played he was working too.

"See," his mother said, smiling. "Now you are a man!"

Soon Nino could walk part of the way home, holding on to his mother's skirt. Along the path across the fields, past the

willows by the edge of the canal, where his mother always held his hand very tightly, and so to the village.

Casa Checchi, where Nino lived with his mother and grandfather, stood on a hill just above the village. A narrow winding path led up to it. The path was steep; it tired Nino's legs, so here his mother always carried him.

When they reached home, Nino's mother prepared the evening meal while Grandfather went to and fro in the courtyard, feeding the pigs, carrying wood and bundles of fagots into the house, and shutting up the chickens in their coop. There was one stubborn old rooster who always gave Grandfather a lot of trouble. Evening after evening he had to chase him around.

"If you don't hop into that coop quick," the old man would say, "tomorrow you will hop into the frying pan!"

[13]

It seemed as if the rooster understood, for at that last threat he would turn, run squawking between Grandfather's legs, and scuttle into the coop with the hens. And Nino, watching from the doorway, would clap his hands and cry: "*Gallo, gallo!*"

Nino liked the bad old *gallo*. He had a *gallo* of his own, a toy rooster which the village priest had given him at his christening, when he was one month old. The colored rooster stood on a shelf above Nino's bed. Nino liked the bright red, white, and green feathers in its tail. There was a whistle hidden under those gay feathers, and when Grandfather or Allinda blew on the whistle the toy rooster would crow.

Next best to the toy *gallo* Nino liked his spoon, which his father had sent him all the way from America. It had a picture on it, a picture of the World's Fair. Nino ate his supper with it every night, sitting on Grandfather's lap at the table.

After supper, when Nino was safely tucked away in his crib, Allinda would work at her loom while Grandfather sat by the fire to smoke his favorite pipe. It was peaceful in the big room; only the soft clatter from the loom broke the stillness at intervals as the heddles were shifted to cross the fine threads and the shuttle went sliding through, back and forth, up and down, the threads weaving closer and tighter with each turn of Allinda's hands. The firelight flickered on the walls, and Nino fell asleep to that soft click and murmur of the shuttle.

One morning when Nino woke, the sun was shining brightly. The house was filled with the early morning smell

[14]

of coffee and woodsmoke. In the kitchen, slices of polenta in neat rows were sizzling on the grate. Allinda had made a big potful the night before. It was corn meal, boiled into a stiff porridge. Nino never tired of it. He liked it best with soft goat cheese and honey spread over it.

"Ancora, ancora!" he begged. "More, more!"

Allinda looked at Grandfather, laughing.

"If we don't take care," she said, "Nino will be eating us out of house and home!"

Grandfather had been up early, looking after the morning chores. Today he was going to the corn field with Allinda and Nino. As he sat down to his breakfast he said: "Nino shouldn't eat so fast. Makes tummy ache." And he poked a finger gently towards Nino's stomach.

But Nino only called for more polenta while he held a bowl of goat's milk in his tiny hands, gulping it down.

Grandfather's eyes twinkled. "Yes," he said, "you'll surely eat us out of house and home, my little Angelino."

Outside in the courtyard, while they waited for Allinda to prepare the noonday lunch, Grandfather said: "Caesar will come along with us today."

Caesar was Grandfather's hunting dog. Nino was very fond of him. Sometimes Grandfather held Nino on Caesar's back for a ride, and that was great fun. But when Nino was alone and Caesar came up in a playful way and licked his face, that Nino didn't like. Then he would yell and make a fuss, and Grandfather would have to come to the rescue.

Nino knew the courtyard from end to end. He knew the

[15]

stone pen where the pigs lived. He knew the chicken coop and would crawl inside it to look for eggs in the straw. He liked the pigs and the hens and Signor Gallo the rooster. But he didn't like the goats that walked about the courtyard butting their heads most of the time, and always making "maa, maa" noises at him.

Allinda came out from the house carrying a bandanna handkerchief knotted at its four corners and bulging with food. Dangling at her side and tied to her waist was a straw-covered bottle filled with red wine. Now they were all ready to go. Nino was wearing the new blue smock which Signora Ditto, his godmother, had made for him. It was the first time he had put it on, and he felt very proud.

Down the winding path, Nino in his blue smock held tight to Allinda's hand, trying hard to keep pace with Grand-father's big steps. Caesar followed closely behind them.

As they walked through the village Nino heard shouts.

"Hello, Nino! My, what a big fellow! And look at that fine new smock," said the cobbler as they passed by.

And the butcher next door called out: "Oh, Nino! Don't work too hard in the fields, and be careful the crows don't get you!"

The village pastrycook, too, saw them coming down the cobbled street. He disappeared into his shop and came out again just in time to give Nino a little bag of candy. Nino smiled and said: "*Grazie*," meaning, "thank you," and began at once to dig down into the bag with his small fingers, repeating: "*Grazie, grazie*," all the while.

[16]

"Listen to him, listen to him," said the good-natured pastrycook. "He talks well now."

"Oh, every day there's a new word—some days three or four. He knows lots of words now, doesn't he?" said Allinda, turning to her father. And she added laughingly: "He doesn't suck his thumb any more, either."

The three walked on. Nino turned every now and then to wave and call out "*Addio*" to the village folks.

"Good-by, Nino," called the pastrycook. "Come and see me soon."

"*Buon' uomo,*" said Nino to his mother. "Good man."

"*Si, Nino, Signor Carlo è un buon' uomo,*" Allinda said.

They walked down the path Grandfather and Allinda knew so well, till they came to the old stone building, like a

[17]

huge barn, which the village people always called "le Cappane." It stood at the edge of the corn fields, and was used to
store hay and grain in harvest time, and to keep the tools that
were used to cultivate the land. While Allinda made her
way to the corn field, Grandfather led Nino into the big
barn. Nino loved the old place. He had spent many hours
there before with his mother, when it was raining too hard
to stay out in the fields. He followed Grandfather about now
while the old man pointed out to him the various implements
that stood leaning against the walls, naming each in turn:
hoes, rakes, flails, scythes, and sickles, and the huge round
sieves. Nino repeated the names after him. Strings of last
year's corn still hung to dry. Onions that sent long green
sprouts upwards like a little forest of young trees stood piled
in a corner, giving the air a musty smell. Nino heard the
crows cawing outdoors, and he too began cawing, his voice
echoing in the large room. Caesar hurried in and out of the
door sniffing the morning air.

Grandfather took his *roncola*, a curved brush-hook with a
short handle, which hung at his belt, and with an iron hammer sharpened its edge on an anvil that stood near the smoky
fireplace.

"Ping, ping, ping," went the hammer.

"Ping, ping, ping," went Nino.

Outside, Nino and Caesar lay and rolled in the tall grass
together while Grandfather cut thin willow saplings for
making fish traps. The old man went about carefully selecting the right sizes and lengths. Then cutting the saplings

[18]

quickly with the *roncola*, he laid them together in neat, long bundles and tied them.

The sun beat down on the corn fields. Allinda was hoeing the earth between the rows of corn. She raised her wet brow and wiped it with the back of her hand. The sun rose higher into the sky. Allinda worked on, piling the earth high around the stalks of corn and leaving a ditch for irrigating. The black crows circled lazily overhead. Now and then she could hear Caesar's barking and Nino's laughter. Allinda was a strong woman and she enjoyed working in the fields. She could work all day long and keep up with the men.

Now the shadows lay almost directly under the tall stalks of corn. It must be almost time to eat lunch, thought Allinda, leaning on the hoe and looking up to the sun. She heard the rustling of corn leaves and saw Nino and Grandfather coming down the rows of corn. Nino was carrying the red handkerchief. It looked like a huge tomato against his blue smock.

"My little man is going to be a great help," said Allinda, taking the red bundle from Nino.

Nino said: "Me strong," and made a gesture as if lifting some unknown heavy object.

Allinda spread the lunch beneath a weeping willow that grew at the edge of the canal, and Nino with a huge piece of bread sat on the bank throwing pebbles into the calm water. He kept himself amused watching the tiny circles spread out into wide, dancing ripples; sometimes the circles broke when they crossed. Schools of fish, mistaking the pebbles for food, swam zigzagging back and forth. Nino threw them bread,

[19]

and the little minnows made fast work of it. Nino laughed.

"All gone, all gone," he said, turning to his mother and pointing to the commotion in the water.

The red, green, and bright blue dragon-flies with long outstretched wings went whirring over Nino's head, sometimes gliding and swooping down as if to alight there. He watched them as they circled, and when one of them swooped too near he waved his arms, saying: "Shush, shush! *Va via!*"

By and by his eyelids began to droop. He fell sound asleep with his head on Allinda's lap.

CHAPTER II

THE BIRTHDAY ROOSTER

N INO stood on a chair beside his mother. She was kneading dough on the lid of a huge oaken chest used to store flour and bread. The lid was covered with flour, and Nino ran his fingers through it, making patterns. Allinda's strong hands rolled the dough; then she pounded it with clenched fists, the flour flying as each blow fell. She pounded and rolled, rolled and pounded.

"Sprinkle a little more flour, Nino. Just a little."

Nino took a handful and sprinkled it over the dough.

Soon the huge lump was ready to be made into loaves. Allinda cut it into six parts with a knife. Nino watched her cut a small piece from one of the larger pieces and put it aside. She patted the rest of the dough into six round loaves.

"See, Nino, six loaves all ready to go into the oven tomorrow morning. One, two, three, four, five, six," said Allinda, touching each loaf in turn.

Nino counted: "One, two, three, four, five, six," and pointing to the small piece his mother had put aside, he said: "and this makes seven."

"Give it to me, Nino. I'll make you a birthday rooster. You will be four tomorrow."

Allinda shaped the dough into a crowing rooster. She patted it gently, flattening it out, while Nino looked on with delight. He danced up and down on the chair and clapped his hands with joy.

"A *gallo*, a *gallo!* Thank you, Mother. Thank you for making me such a splendid rooster."

Allinda placed the six loaves on a long oaken board, and covered them over with a thick woolen blanket. She lifted one corner of the blanket.

"See, Nino, we must put Signor Gallo to sleep for the night, and by tomorrow he will have grown to twice his size. You'll see," said Allinda.

Nino could hardly wait until tomorrow to see how big the rooster would have grown.

He peeked under the blanket and said: "*Buona notte*, Signor Gallo—good night, Mr. Rooster."

"Nino, you are a sight! Your grandfather will think you have fallen into the flour barrel," Allinda said as she washed

Nino's face and hands, and then went to prepare the evening meal.

Nino kept peeking under the woolen blanket every little while to see if the rooster had grown any larger.

Grandfather came into the house with a string of little green frogs. He had caught them in the marsh.

"They're just the right size for frying," he said to Allinda.

Allinda cleaned, floured, and fried the frogs. They ate them with corn meal porridge, soft goat's milk cheese, and a salad of dandelions. Nino had a bowl of hot porridge with milk and sugar. He barely tasted the frogs.

Before going off to bed he looked under the woolen blanket once more.

"Sh," he said. "Mr. Rooster is sound asleep."

Next morning Nino awoke early. He rushed down the stairs before anyone was up and, making straight for the covered loaves, he lifted the blanket.

"Oh, my! Oh, my! How you have grown! You have swollen to twice the size, just as Mother said you would. You're nearly as large as Grandfather's rooster now," said Nino. "Oh, my!" And he went back to bed.

After breakfast Grandfather heated the outdoor oven, which was built of bricks and large enough for two Ninos to have crawled inside it. He made the fire right on the oven floor, laying a fagot of brushwood first, then some larger sticks on top. When the fire had begun to burn and crackle he closed the oven door and went off to his work in the marshes. Allinda watched the fire, and when it had burned down to red coals she raked the glowing embers carefully to the sides of the oven, swept the brick floor in the middle clean of ashes, and went to fetch the loaves.

Nino saw his mother coming towards the oven, carrying the long board on her head.

"Be careful of Mr. Rooster," he called. "Don't drop him."

Allinda placed the board down near the oven and with a sharp knife cut a cross on each loaf; on the rooster she cut wings and a tail.

"He is a splendid rooster, Mother. Will he get any bigger?"

"He will be twice as big when he comes out of the oven after baking," said Allinda, "and he will be good and brown too. A fine-looking rooster he'll be!"

She lifted each loaf on the long paddle, made the sign of the cross, and placed them on the hot bricks in the oven.

"One, two, three, four, five, six," counted Nino as each loaf went in. "Now it's time for Mr. Rooster," he said, giving it a last farewell touch.

"Yes, it's Signor Gallo's turn to cook, now. In he goes," said Allinda. "He will be out soon, Nino. It won't take long to cook him."

She lifted Nino up to see the loaves in the oven. Right in the center lay Mr. Rooster. He already seemed to be puffing himself up as if to crow. The wooden door, padded with a dampened cloth, was shut tight, and the long paddle propped up against it to keep it from falling open. Nino saw the white steam rise around the door. It floated upward and was lost in the grape arbor that sheltered the oven. From the house, the oven looked like a huge egg half buried in the courtyard. Nino sat on the doorstep wondering when his mother would take Mr. Rooster out of the hot oven. As he sat musing, his grandfather came across the courtyard.

"Hello, Nino," he said. "What are you thinking about?"

"*Gallo è in forno*. Rooster's in the oven," said Nino, pointing. "Mother put him in this morning. He is cooking now."

"Rooster is in the oven? What rooster, Nino?" cried the old man in alarm. "What rooster? Allinda," he called through the door, "what's this about a rooster in the oven? You didn't—did you? You know I'm saving him for Easter. You're not baking my pet rooster, are you?"

Allinda came to the door, laughing. She had heard the conversation.

"Oh, no, Grandfather. Nino means the rooster I made for him from bread dough. It's in the oven now."

She laughed and Nino laughed too. Grandfather's pet rooster crowed loudly from the top of the long grape arbor. The old man took out his handkerchief and wiped his brow.

"I was afraid," he said, "that you were cooking my rooster. You know, Allinda, I am sparing him until Easter. Thank goodness," he said as he entered the house.

From the doorstep Nino watched the goats and hens in a corner of the courtyard. The live Mr. Gallo had flown down from the arbor and now strutted among the flock of hens, scratching the ground and clucking, sending them scattering in all directions.

[25]

Grandfather was sharpening his *roncola*. They were all
going up on the hillside below the monastery to gather
fagots. Allinda had swept the flagged floor and was now
washing it with a broom made of dry grass tied fast together
with hempen cords.

"I think the bread is about done, Nino. We'll see how
large Signor Gallo is now," she said.

Nino sprang to his feet and ran to the oven.

"Open the door quickly, Mother. Take him out first," he
said, jumping up and down.

Allinda reached into the hot oven with the long paddle
and took out the rooster, now grown to twice his size and
nice and brown.

"Cock-a-doodle-do!" cried Nino. "He is a full-grown
rooster now. May I hold him, Mother?"

"*Troppo caldo.* It's too hot, Nino. You may have him after
he has cooled."

Allinda reached into the oven again and one by one she

[26]

took out the brown loaves. The crisscross on each had baked into a rich thick crust. She set the loaves on a long oaken board and carried them into the house. The fragrance of the new bread filled the room, and Grandfather left off sharpening his *roncola* to look.

"A fine smell, Allinda," he said. "The new flour is good!"

Gingerly he held Nino's rooster in his hands.

"*Bellissimo gallo*. M-m. Smells good too." And he handed it to Nino. "Here take it," he said. "It's yours. Wait until it cools before you eat it."

Wearing his new smock, Nino walked between Allinda and his grandfather. Above them stood the monastery, like a ruined castle, gray and somber in the morning light. Nino held the bread rooster tightly in his hand. Every now and then he took a bite.

"Its head is gone already," Grandfather said.

Chestnut, hazel, and cypress trees and rich green shrubs covered the hillside along the path. Quail flew up, startled by the sound of footsteps, and Nino turned to watch them disappear into the brush. The air was filled with the cooing of wild doves, and the brook that flowed along the path murmured pleasantly.

As they approached a steep incline that led to a level spot on the hillside, Grandfather lifted Nino into his arms, and said: "We will soon be there. Save some of that rooster for later on. You will be hungry."

Nino tucked what was left into his pocket and gave his grandfather a tight hug.

[27]

Now they could hear the sharp blows of a *roncola* and the crash of falling brush, together with a man's voice singing. They climbed higher and higher. The path became steeper as they went.

"Sounds like Signor Ditto's voice," said Grandfather to Allinda. Signor Ditto was their neighbor, and Nino's godfather.

"You can always tell Signor Ditto's voice, especially when he sings," said Allinda. "He's up bright and early today."

"If it's Signor Ditto, Julio will be there too," said Nino. "We can play together, can't we, Mother?"

Julio, Signor Ditto's little boy, was just Nino's own age, and the two were close playmates.

When they reached the stretch of level ground, there was Signor Ditto singing at the top of his voice as he slashed at the brush. An armful fell with each stroke of his heavy, curved blade. Signor Ditto always did everything very energetically.

"*Buon giorno, Signor Ditto!*" Grandfather shouted. "You are up here early this morning."

"*Buon giorno, Padrone,*" answered Signor Ditto. "Not much to do down below. Best to cut while the cutting is good."

He pointed with his *roncola* towards a huge pile of fagots. Then, picking Nino up, he gave him a fatherly hug. Nino held out the half-eaten rooster.

"Have some, Signor Ditto. It's good. Mother made it this morning. Gallo is almost all gone now. Have some?"

[28]

Signor Ditto chuckled as he put the little boy down. "Your appetite grows with you, Nino," he said. "Eat away! It will make you big and strong."

Allinda walked towards Signora Ditto, who was sitting on a boulder beside a shallow pool of clear water, crocheting lace. The Signora was fat and kind and middle-aged, with a beaming, good-natured face. She was so stout that she had quite a struggle before she managed to get up to shake hands with Allinda. The Signora shook your hand even if you had met her only two hours ago. She excelled every woman in the village with her good manners and extreme politeness.

All the while she talked with Allinda the fat Signora's hands flew over the lace like lightning, never pausing, never dropping a stitch.

"How is Nino? And Grandfather? Have you heard from

America? Is Nino's father coming home soon? Or will he send for you?" Seeing Nino, she said: "Hello, Nino. Come here. Let me see how the new smock fits."

"Hello, Maria." Nino always called the Signora by her first name. "Where is Julio? Didn't he come with you today?"

"Oh, Nino!" came a voice from behind a wild-rose bush near the brook.

It was Julio's voice.

"Oh, Nino, come on in. The water is fine," he said, as he jumped and splashed about naked and waist-deep in a clear pool.

Nino took off his shoes and smock and, holding the remains of the rooster in one hand, walked into the pool. Bright pebbles sparkled under the clear water. Moss-covered stones and water cress edged the pool. The overhanging trees shaded the water at one end, turning it to a deep dark green. The brook, flowing between two huge boulders, sang an endless rippling song.

Nino gave what was left of the rooster to Julio, who made short work of it, devouring it in one mouthful. The two boys splashed about the pool with glee.

They jumped up and down, crying out: "I'll beat you to the other end!"

Allinda sat beside the fat Signora. They talked while Grandfather and Signor Ditto continued cutting fagots. A flock of sparrows flew from tree to tree, and there was a faint sound of tinkling bells from the herd of goats grazing higher up on the hillside. The sunshine was very warm and bright.

"Nino is four today, Signora. Think of it. Doesn't time fly?" said Allinda.

"And my Julio is four today, too. It doesn't seem half as long as that since Julio was born. Time does fly, Allinda! It's one thing we can't stop," said the fat Signora, complacently.

The fact that her boy had been born on the same day as Nino made a strong bond between her and Allinda. Ever since that singular occurrence they had become inseparable friends.

Noon hour came and with it the sound of the village church bells. Grandfather and Signor Ditto tied their fagots into bundles with thin green withes.

"Did you have good luck with your fishing, Padrone?" asked Signor Ditto, as he bound his last fagots tightly.

"Very good. I caught the largest mess of frogs in a long time," said Grandfather. "The fishing was splendid early this morning. Just before sunrise, I caught the biggest carp you ever saw. It was this big." He spread his hands wide apart as he spoke. "It is a surprise for Allinda. She doesn't know that I caught it. Signor Ditto, it's too big for us to eat alone. I want you, the Signora, and Julio to stay with us for dinner tonight. It's Nino's and Julio's birthday and we may as well celebrate it with baked carp. Allinda will certainly bake the carp when she sees how big it is."

"And Allinda knows how to bake carp, too. We shall be happy to dine at your house, Padrone," said Signor Ditto.

"I haven't had a well-cooked carp since I can remember."

The two men made their way towards a huge chestnut tree. Under the shade of its wide-spreading branches, Allinda and Signora Ditto were setting out the lunch. Nino sat beside Grandfather, who was eating a huge red onion. The mere sight of it caused tears to come into Nino's eyes and he sneezed twice while his mouth was full of cheese.

"It's so good to have company for lunch," said Allinda.

"And it's good to have the same company for dinner too," said Grandfather with a wink towards Signor Ditto. "A fine carp dinner would taste good, no? I have invited the Dittos for one of your good carp dinners, Allinda. What do you think?"

"Oh, that's splendid, Father. But, but, the carp? How do you know that you can catch one in time for dinner?"

Grandfather could not keep his secret any longer.

"The carp is at home now. The biggest you ever saw, Allinda. Oh, it's a big one! I cleaned it and put it under two stones in the brook, where it will keep fresh. Wait till you see it. You'll all agree that it's the biggest fish that has been caught in a long time," he said proudly.

"I think Father is joking," said Allinda to Signora Ditto.

"If he isn't joking he is bragging. He told me the fish was this long," said Signor Ditto, and he mimicked Grandfather's description by spreading his arms straight out on either side of him.

Nino threw bread crumbs to the sparrows who came so near that Julio tried to catch one of them. After lunch the men stretched out on the grass in the cool shade of the huge tree. They lay in silence, each staring up into the green foliage above.

"The chestnut flour is getting low, but there will be plenty of nuts this year," said Signor Ditto presently.

Grandfather stroked his long white mustache and replied: "It will be a good year all around, Ditto. The corn crop looks better than it has in years. There will be plenty of everything."

He yawned and added: "Didn't I catch the biggest fish this year, too?"

The two boys had gone in search of mushrooms. Allinda and the fat Signora sat gossiping in low tones for fear of awakening the men, who had dozed off to sleep. The afternoon wore on. The meadow, green and fresh with luxuriant growth, was a quiet haven. Only the singing of the birds, the low murmur of the brook above the pool, and an occasional yell or shout from the boys broke the silence.

The sun, slanting slowly towards the west, hung like a ball of fire over the village and the lowlands. Heat waves danced over the corn and rice fields, and a soft haze hid the horizon. The two boys climbed higher up the hillside.

"Isn't it quiet up here?" said Julio. "There's hardly a sound."

"Oh, I hear lots of things," said Nino. "The brook and the birds, and the bells. They come from Gobo's goats. He must be above us not far from here. Let's go up a little farther, Julio. Maybe Gobo will tell us a story."

[33]

"I hope we don't get lost; then we couldn't have any carp, and besides we would have to sleep up here in the dark. I wouldn't like that a bit," said Julio, almost ready to turn back at the thought.

"Oh, no, we can't get lost. See the big chestnut tree below? We can find our way back by that."

After much climbing through underbrush and over boulders they reached the gentle slope beneath the monastery, quite out of breath. The old building loomed above them like a huge stone wall, looking almost as if it were about to tumble down on their heads. Gobo, a little old man with white whiskers and a shiny bald head, was asleep on a boulder. He looked like a gnome lying curled up there in the sun with his knees almost touching his chin. The herd of goats was gathered near him.

"Too bad, Julio. No story. He's asleep, and I don't dare to wake him up. The last time I did that, he was terribly

[34]

angry. Let's fill his hat with mushrooms and then he will be surprised when he wakes up."

Moving on tiptoe, they searched for the flat mushrooms that grew here and there, looking like round white stones on the short pasture turf. When they had gathered a handful, they stole up and dropped them into the old man's hat, scurrying away with giggles. As they scrambled down the hillside again, they heard the voice of Signor Ditto echoing on the air.

"We can't get lost if your father keeps on singing," said Nino.

A hedgehog scurried for cover as the two boys went hurriedly down the slope. By the time they reached the meadow they were out of breath. Signor Ditto and Grandfather had tied the bundles of fagots together with rope and now two huge heaps stood on the ground.

"We saw Gobo, Mother," said Nino.

"Any stories?"

"No, Mother, he was fast asleep."

"He sleeps all the time, Nino. I never knew a man who could sleep as much as Gobo does. He is half asleep when he comes to the village selling his goat's milk cheese. Some day he will be carried home dead from sleep!" And Allinda laughed.

Grandfather and Signor Ditto, each with a huge load of fagots, made their way down the path. The women and the two boys followed them. Signor Ditto sang cheerfully, while the huge load of fagots bobbed up and down as he walked.

When the little group finally reached Casa Checchi, the sun was setting over the lowlands. It threw a golden splendor over the marshes and fields. The gentle evening breeze cooled the hot faces of the two men.

"There," said Grandfather, throwing down his load beside the oven. "That will keep the fire going for another week.

"Now I'll show you all a real fish," he said as he disappeared through a stone archway that led to the path to the brook. When he came back, his face was beaming with pride.

Everyone looked at the huge carp, without head or tail, and exclaimed: "Oh!"

Nino said: "Oh, oh, a big, big fish! Grandfather, he is heavy, isn't he?"

He touched the wet fish with one finger.

"By the luck of Jonah, he is a whopper, indeed, Padrone! At first I thought you were bragging. It's the biggest fish I ever saw around these parts, but it will be only a fish story to the village folks unless they see it," said Signor Ditto.

"It will make a fine dinner," said Allinda, throwing two small bundles of fagots into the oven. She lighted them and went into the house to prepare the huge carp for baking.

Signora Ditto followed Allinda about the house.

"Let me help you. I must have something to do."

Finally Allinda let Signora Ditto start the fire in the big fireplace, and hang the black pot over it filled with water for the corn meal polenta. While the water boiled, Signor Ditto and Julio made their way home down the hill to feed their

stock. The Dittos' stock consisted of four goats, six pigs, a
lazy rooster, a small flock of scraggling hens, some pigeons
that spent most of their time flying to and from the church
belfry, and, last of all, Bimbo, the little donkey who, when
not pulling the cart, stood lazily about the courtyard. Signor
Ditto's pride and joy was his vineyard and wine cellar. He
did not own as much land as Nino's grandfather, but what
with the selling of wine and hauling with the donkey cart,
the Dittos lived comfortably.

Allinda rubbed the huge fish well with garlic and olive oil.
She placed it in an iron skillet. Then she spread over it finely
chopped rosemary, thyme, sage, and fresh green parsley from
the garden. Mushrooms and tomatoes and dried peppers

[37]

would be added later. Nino stood beside his mother as she prepared the fish for the oven. The fragrance of the herbs made his nose twitch, and the odor of garlic reminded him of the day when he was ill and his mother had made a necklace of garlic to hang around his neck.

Grandfather finished feeding the pigs and came into the house.

"It smells good already," he said, looking at the fish. "At any rate he looks better than he did this morning."

"It's ready for the oven now, Father," said Allinda. "Will you put it in? I'll make the polenta. Come, Nino, bring me the corn meal."

Slowly Allinda poured the meal into the boiling water, stirring as she poured. Soon the porridge thickened and Nino heard the blub-a-blub-blub of the meal as it boiled and sputtered. Allinda left the stirring to Signora Ditto who sat on a stool and stirred slowly with a long wooden stick.

A jovial voice rang across the courtyard, and Nino ran to the door. He saw Signor Ditto and Julio returning to the house. Signor Ditto walked with long swaggering strides, singing at the top of his voice and carrying a large bottle in either hand.

"Here comes Signor Ditto now!" cried Nino.

"I can hear him, Nino," said Allinda with a broad smile on her face, and she looked towards the fat Signora.

"That man never gets tired of singing. Sometimes he even sings in his sleep," said the jovial Signora as she went on stirring the polenta.

[38]

Allinda, with a bowl of conserva—the stiff, home-made tomato paste—and some sliced mushrooms, went to the oven. She spread the tomato over the steaming fish and arranged the mushrooms around it.

"Pretty soon now, Nino," she said. "Pretty soon it will be ready."

On their way back to the house Nino stopped to point to the sky. "Guarda il bel cielo!" he said.

The two stood for a moment gazing. A deep pink glowed behind the gray walls of the house. A flock of pigeons flew overhead, black against the sunset, and, making a sudden turn as though startled, disappeared into the green hillside below the monastery. Nino thought of Gobo, and wondered if he was still asleep up there on his boulder.

They went into the house and found Signor Ditto already pouring wine into the glasses. The newly lighted candles spluttered and flickered a moment, then burned with a smooth steady glow. Now and then the flame swayed, making shadows dance on the whitewashed walls. The room felt restful, filled with an atmosphere of friendliness, deep and silent.

Allinda lifted the heavy pot from the fire and poured the hot polenta onto a napkin spread ready on the table. It was thick and steaming, and the huge lump showed a golden yellow under the candlelight. Everyone sat down to the table except Allinda, who had gone to the oven to fetch the carp.

Nino watched his grandfather serve the polenta. It was

[39]

an operation that always interested him. Grandfather took a thin string, and holding the two ends between the thumb and forefinger of each hand he stretched the string taut, then sank it carefully through the polenta. Five times he did this, ending with one long cut down the middle. When he had finished, the huge lump fell apart, neatly divided so that twelve steaming slices lay there on the napkin. It was like magic.

Everyone drew a long breath as Allinda set the platter of baked fish on the table. The carp was a reddish brown color, surrounded by its rich sauce, and the seasoning had formed a delicious savory crust. Grandfather, sitting at the head of the table, served a slice of polenta and a portion of the fish to each one.

Then he said the "Our Father" aloud.

Signor Ditto said: "Nino, you are lucky to have a mother who can cook so well!"

Grandfather lifted his glass. "*Salute, buon' salute e buona fortuna!* Good health and good luck!"

They drank the deep red wine while Julio and Nino held up their cups of goat's milk. "*Salute, salute!*" they repeated, laughing.

"A good vintage, Signor Ditto. A very excellent vintage," said Grandfather, smacking his lips, and holding the glass to the candlelight he added: "Look, Nino. Did you ever see such a beautiful color? Oh, it's like a ruby, it's magnificent!"

Signor Ditto, who always liked to hear his wine praised, beamed with pleasure.

[40]

"It is a good wine, even if I say so myself." He added politely: "But this carp tastes much better to me."

He turned to Allinda. "I hope you will tell Maria your secret for cooking carp. The polenta is good too. The Genoese eat a lot of polenta; they know what's good. Do you know, Padrone," he said to Grandfather, "that the poorer peasants in the province hang a roasted smoked bloater from the ceiling and let the juice drip down on the polenta? Yes, I've heard my own father tell me," he went on earnestly, while Grandfather smiled, for he had heard this old joke about the Genoese before. "They sit round, all eating like savages, and when the polenta is all gone they draw lots for the bloater. Sometimes they come to blows over it."

Allinda was telling Signora Ditto about all the different ways she knew of cooking fish.

"Mother cooks frogs so you can eat heads, legs, and all," Nino put in. "She knows how to keep the eels from jumping out of the frying pan, too."

They ate heartily and Signor Ditto drank a considerable quantity of his own wine.

"I don't know what you have done to the fish, Allinda. It tastes better than any you have ever cooked."

"It's the white wine Signor Ditto gave me last year, Grandfather. I poured a little over the carp just after I took it out of the oven. That's my secret for cooking carp. It makes it taste different."

"I have heard tell of a way to cook carp that is different from any other," Signor Ditto said, "and even you will admit, Allinda, that it is different when you hear it."

"Tell us, Signor Ditto. I'd like very much to know. Perhaps I might cook it that way the next time you come. Please tell us."

"Well," said Signor Ditto, "I will tell you."

He put on a very solemn face, winked slyly at Grandfather, and, leaning far back in his chair, he began. "Remember, this is a special recipe and it is not known by everyone. So listen carefully, and you won't ever forget it.

"You must have a good-sized carp first of all. Oh, say the size of the one Grandfather caught this morning; in other words, like the one we have just eaten," he went on. "About that size would do. After cleaning it well, you must garnish it with all the flavorings that Allinda used in cooking this one tonight. The finer the seasoning, the better the taste. It has been said that the most important part of cooking is the preparation of the food. Fire will do the rest. The carp is now cleaned and garnished," said Signor Ditto, waving his hands grandly in illustration. "You then place it upon a flat piece of wet clay."

Everyone looked surprised. They glanced at one another.

"You then wrap the fish up in the clay, and seal it up tightly."

Signor Ditto went through all the movements with his hands.

"Now the carp is ready for cooking," he said.

Nino sat listening open-mouthed.

"Then it is put in the oven."

[43]

They all waited patiently for the imaginary baking to be done, while Signor Ditto poured himself another glass of wine.

"After the clay with the carp wrapped up in it has been left in the oven, say, for an hour or an hour and a quarter, it is taken out. By this time the soft clay has hardened almost to stone. It is placed on the table. You sit down to eat. You break open the clay, take out the carp carefully, oh, very carefully. Then you throw it away and eat the clay. That's the way I have heard tell of cooking carp," said Signor Ditto.

Everyone shouted with laughter, and Signor Ditto, quite overcome by the success of his story, held his sides while the tears rolled down his cheeks.

Allinda said: "Is it really a true story, Signor Ditto? Did it really happen? Does one actually eat the clay?"

"Yes, and it tastes good, too, Allinda," said Grandfather, between fits of laughter.

Nino and Julio, hearing all the merriment, laughed louder than anyone else.

"More, more stories!" they cried.

Caesar crawled out from under the table and sat in the middle of the floor, his bright kindly eyes blinking as he looked from one to another. Signora Ditto, fat and flushed, pointed a reproving finger at her husband. Allinda went to the cupboard and brought cheese, apples, pomegranates, and a bowl of nuts, and set a pot of black coffee on the table.

"Please, Grandfather, will you tell us a story now? Signor Ditto told one," Nino begged.

Julio, sitting across the table from Nino, said: "Your grandfather tells good stories. Nino."

Grandfather had broken a pomegranate and sat picking out the tiny lustrous kernels. One by one, they disappeared rapidly as he flipped them into his mouth. He sat for a moment.

"I know a story you might like to hear," he said finally.

"Oh, goody, goody!" cried Nino. "Make it a long, long story, won't you, Grandfather? A long, long one this time."

"It's not about gypsies, nor is it about fairies," said Grandfather. "It is a story about something that actually happened right here in this village. It happened when I was a boy about the age of ten. I can remember the whole thing quite plainly." He thought a moment, then took out his pipe, lighting it with a long sulphur match. Then he began the story of *The Rakka Box*.

CHAPTER III

THE RAKKA BOX

"I CAN remember that day very well," Grandfather began. "It was early in the morning, and my father and I were just getting ready to take the goats up on the hillside, when we heard a lot of shouting and hubbub going on down in the village. Father said:

" 'There must be something wrong. Maybe the Mayor has called a meeting. Let's go down and find out what's the matter.'

"So we hurried down the hill to the village square, and there we found everyone gathered together. Father asked what all the excitement was about. Everybody was talking at once, but at last someone told him: 'It's a miracle man. He's got some sort of a magic box and he says it will work miracles.'

"Father held me tightly by the hand, and we pushed through the crowd, and there we saw the miracle man, as they called him. He was a poorly dressed man with red hair and a rusty-colored face; he looked as if he might have been a Venetian. Anyway, he was a stranger to us. He had a little box in his hand and he was talking to the crowd.

" 'My dear friends,' he was saying, 'I have brought you a gift from God.' And he held the box up so that everyone could see it. It was a small box with a little handle on one side.

"The crowd all began craning their heads like so many chickens. Someone asked: 'What is it? A mouse trap?' The man shook his head.

" 'This little box, my friends,' he said, 'will perform wonders. It is a rain maker. When you want rain, all you have to do is to turn this little crank on the side here, and the rain will fall.'

"He turned the handle, just a little. It made a queer rattling noise—rakka, rakka, rakka—so loud that everyone near him jumped. They looked up at the sky. It was clear as crystal. Not a cloud was in sight.

" 'Rakka, rakka, rakka,' went the box again. Nothing happened.

"Someone back in the crowd shouted: 'Show us, show us!

[47]

If you say the box can work a miracle, show us!' And the rest of the people all began to mumble and murmur. They too wanted to see something happen. But the red-haired man merely smiled.

" 'It will perform the miracle,' he said solemnly, 'only when the miracle is needed. Now I am just showing you all how it works.' He cranked the box again. This time he turned the handle faster and the noise was louder still. It sounded as if a thousand frogs were croaking all at once. It was a terrible noise. Rakka, rakka, rakka! It frightened the children in the crowd and they began crying: 'Waa, waa, waa!' "

Grandfather paused a moment. He looked at the two little boys, who were all excited.

"What happened, Grandfather?" Nino asked. "What happened? Tell us!"

"The man stopped cranking the box. He lifted one hand, and spoke.

" 'I have traveled,' he began, 'all over the country.' He took out a dirty red handkerchief and blew his long nose. It sounded like the blast of a trumpet. 'I have traveled all over the country, to help the people save their crops from drought and their animals from famine.' Once more he held the box up on high. 'This,' he said, 'this is what will work the miracle. No more need for buckets and water-wheels—no more need to break your backs working all day in the hot sun to irrigate your corn and wheat fields! You shall see,' he said, 'what this box will do for you. Step right up close now, friends, and I will show you how it is made. There is no secret; it works on

[48]

the great principle of science. It is a simple box, very simple, and anyone can make it.'

"Some of the country folk began now to get really interested, but others in the crowd shook their fists and jeered at the red-haired man, calling him a trickster. The red-haired man paid no attention to them. He went on explaining how the box was made. Lifting the lid, he showed them a sort of paddle-wheel inside it, with blades that struck against a flat bit of steel when the handle was turned. This was what made the noise.

" 'Just a simple box,' he kept saying. 'You can make it of thin, well-seasoned wood and a flat piece of steel. An old kitchen knife blade will do very well.'

"Everyone studied the box, inside and out, their eyes almost popping out of their heads. They could see for themselves how simple it was to make, just as the red-haired man had said. Meantime the red-haired man had begun to move about among the crowd, holding out his hat. People dropped pennies into it.

" 'Remember,' he went on, 'the box must be made of thin, well-seasoned wood, and you must use it only in times of drought.'

"Soon his hat was heaped up with coppers. Some of the more ignorant peasants, who were so stupid they would believe anything one told them, even dropped silver in as they pressed forward for a closer look at the precious box. Everyone began chattering at once, like a nest of magpies, and while they were busy talking and arguing among themselves the red-haired man emptied his money into his pockets, put his hat on his head, and disappeared with his box under his arm. No one ever saw or heard of him again. Not in our village, anyway."

Nino drew a long breath.

"Tell us another story, Grandfather," he said. "That one wasn't long enough."

"Patience, Nino, patience. Wait a minute. I haven't finished this one yet."

Grandfather lit his pipe again, and continued. "A great many of the villagers really did make the little boxes just as the man had told them. They took the best-seasoned wood they could find, they hunted up their old broken kitchen knives, and when the boxes were done they looked very fine. Some even had carving and designs on them. A few people actually hoped that a drought would come, they were so impatient to try out their boxes and see what would happen. But meanwhile there was no need for rain; things went on as usual, the crops were good and little by little the craze about the rakka boxes died down. Some people even began to feel a little ashamed that they had spent so much time and trouble over them; they put their boxes away in the closet and forgot all about them.

"Two years passed since the day the miracle man had come to the village. And then there came a year when there was very little rain and hardly any snow. Everything began to suffer from the lack of water. The corn and wheat dwindled in the fields; the grass was only as high as your hand. The grape vines and olive trees bore no fruit. Wells began to dry up, and still the hot sun beat down. Day after day the village folk looked up into the sky for a sign of rain.

" 'If it would only rain,' they said, 'perhaps the crops might be saved yet.'

"The priest announced special masses to pray for rain, but still no rain fell. The people began to murmur.

[51]

"And then they remembered the rakka boxes. Someone said: 'Why not give the rakka box a test? After all, the miracle man said it was a gift from God.'

"So they fetched their rakka boxes out. The peasants took them into the fields, and all day long they cranked and cranked—'rakka, rakka, rakka'—till the very crows flapped round in frightened circles overhead.

" 'Rakka, rakka, rakka.'

"From all over the lowlands sounded the noise of the boxes. It could be heard for miles around. It sounded as if all the frogs in the world had gathered to croak in chorus. The village priest was angry; he said that the people were taking up with magic and no good could come of it; but he

could not make them stop. He said his masses for rain and the people all came to church and prayed, but all through the week they cranked their rakka boxes just the same.

"For thirty days and thirty nights the 'rakka, rakka, rakka' never ceased. Still there was no sign of rain; not even a tiny cloud was to be seen in the clear sky. One day the villagers became very, very angry. Some of them smashed their rakka boxes; others were too tired to turn the handles any longer. They shook their fists at the sky, chewed on their knuckles, and cursed the rakka man.

"One of the villagers said: 'Perhaps we did not make the boxes just the way the miracle man said we should.'

"Others said: 'Perhaps we have not been patient enough.'

"And then the rakka boxes started all over again. It was as if the whole world had gone mad. The villagers seemed bent on cranking for the rest of their lives. And then one day a cloud rose with the morning sun.

"By noon that day the sky was overcast. A pale gray mist gathered and hung over the village, and by night it had begun to rain. The rakka boxes were working at last!

"At first it rained gently. The village folk caressed their rakka boxes. Hadn't they worked a miracle, just as the man said? The people prayed and gave thanks for the falling rain.

"It rained and rained. By midnight it was a deluge. The villagers, snug in their homes, sang happy songs about the rakka boxes. The miracle man had been right after all. Now there need be no more fear for the future. They could have rain whenever they wanted it.

"And for ten days," said Grandfather solemnly, "it rained without ceasing. Every morning the people stuck their heads out of window, only to see torrents of water streaming down from the dark gray clouds. Rain they had wanted, and rain they got. But this was too much of a good thing. Candles burned in the houses, and people hurried through the downpour wrapped in sheepskin coats. The roads about the village flowed like rivers as the water drained off to the lowlands.

" 'Perhaps we overworked the rakka boxes,' someone suggested. 'Who knows?'

"By day and by night the rain fell. If it did not stop soon, the entire country would be under water. The lowlands were already flooded and the peasants who lived there had to move to the village. As many as four or five families were crowded into one house. People were in despair. They prayed and prayed. Kneeling in barns and wet homes, the peasants prayed. They prayed kneeling among cattle and sheep, pigs and babies, sick grandfathers and chattering grandmothers. And, believe me, they prayed in earnest!

"On the twelfth day the rain ceased and the sun broke through. Gray clouds lined with silver swirled overhead, and when they saw those clouds a wail of relief, almost a roar, rose from every house in the village, making nearly as much noise as the rakka boxes had done.

"The clouds scattered, and deep blue sky showed through. The water in the streets disappeared and the folk ventured out, feeling dazed like people who had been in prison. The

lowlands below Casa Checchi had disappeared and a muddy
sea of water and wreckage lay where once had been rich fields
of wheat and corn. Only the topmost branches of the poplars
along the canal showed like bushes floating on the surface.
As far as eye could see the country was flooded.

"The church bells rang out, loud and joyous, calling the
people to prayer. The musty smell of wet clothes and incense
filled the crowded church as they knelt and prayed, giving
thanks to God for bringing the sun back to them. But when
mass was over and the people moved slowly out of the
church, the sky was again overcast and misty drops began to
fall. In despair the villagers looked up to the heavens. Was
this never going to end? Amid their praying and weeping
the rain fell faster and faster.

"Then the priest in his altar robes stood on the steps of the
church and with uplifted hands called the people back into
the church. In silence they made their way up the steps, and
in silence they knelt again. From the pulpit the priest spoke
to them, gravely and sternly.

" 'Our Lord who is in heaven has been vexed,' he said.
'He has seen the evil caused by your cursed rakka boxes. You
have lost your faith in the Lord, and therefore He has seen
fit to punish you. My good people,' he said, 'go home and
destroy the rakka boxes. Burn them! The Lord will look
down and He will be pleased to see your faith in Him restored. Only God is a worker of miracles. No living mortal
can equal His work, and the mortal that thinks he can perform miracles by means of a wooden box is either a charlatan

[55]

or is possessed of the devil. Go and destroy the evil boxes!'

"The villagers made the sign of the cross, hanging their

heads in penitence. The rain fell in torrents as they hurried home to burn their rakka boxes. And all through that night the storm raged. Thunder and lightning crashed, huge hailstones fell on the tiled roofs, making a rattle louder than a million rakka boxes. The hail broke the tiles and windows, it tore the leaves, and ripped the bark off trees. To the frightened peasants it seemed that the anger of God was about to destroy them utterly. But by midnight the rain had subsided; only the wind still whistled and howled round the houses. By dawn the sky was clear and the hills showed sharp against a pale sulphur sky. Still terrified, the people peered through their windows as the light increased and saw the sun rise slowly and majestically above the golden clouds. The storm had ended.

"And that," said Grandfather, "is the end of the rakka box story, as it is known."

The little group sat round the table in silence. The candles had burned low and the fire flickered lazily.

"Did everyone burn up their rakka boxes, Grandfather?" asked Nino.

"No, Nino, apparently not. Because one day years ago, before you were born, while I was cleaning out the loft at 'le Cappane,' I found one poked away high up in the rafters. I brought it home and it's upstairs in the attic now. Would you like to see a rakka box?" he asked them all.

Nino clapped his hands in excitement.

"Oh, please, Grandfather, do show it to us. You'd like to see it, wouldn't you, Julio?"

[57]

"Do get it, do get it!" Julio cried.

Grandfather took one of the candles from the table and went upstairs. Presently he returned, holding a square wooden box under his arm. Setting it on the floor, he said: "There you are. This is one of the infernal things that caused all the mischief in this village when I was ten years old."

Nino and Julio walked around the box curiously, touching first one side, then the other. It didn't look like anything very terrible. Nino was puzzled.

"It looks just like any ordinary box, doesn't it, Julio?"

"Oh, but it isn't," said Grandfather. "Just you wait a minute." And he took hold of the little crank on the side of the box and began to turn it. Instantly a harsh rattling noise filled the room. It was horrid—worse than the croaking of any frogs that ever lived. The boys held their hands tightly over their ears. Signor Ditto shouted: "Stop it, stop it! Santa Maria, help us!" and crossed himself hurriedly. "Stop it, Padrone. Stop the infernal thing!"

But Grandfather went on cranking the box and roaring with laughter as he turned the handle faster and faster. Allinda and the fat Signora sat as if nailed to their chairs. Caesar lifted his head and barked and howled in chorus with the racket.

"Oh, please, Father! Take it back upstairs!" Allinda cried at last. "It might bring on a storm the way it did in your story."

Signor Ditto was really scared. He stared in horror at the box and yelled at Grandfather: "Burn the infernal thing!

[58]

Get rid of it, if there is any truth to your story. You are sheltering an evil invention. Throw it into the fire. Burn it up. You're driving us all frantic!" And he shook his clasped hands in the air.

Nino stood with his mouth open, staring. What was in that box? Could it really be frogs? Grandfather, still shaking with laughter, stopped the horrible racket. He picked the rakka box up and took it back to the attic. Nino could hear him still chuckling and laughing as his heavy shoes went clump, clump up the stairs.

That night as Nino lay in his bed the moonbeams made a pale half-light in the room. He could hear the "rakka, rakka, rakka" of the frogs down in the marshes. "Rakka, rakka, rakka," came the voices. They grew fainter, and fainter still. Nino lay snug in his bed, and the colored toy rooster sat silently on the shelf above him.

CHAPTER IV

THE PICTURE

Nino was going to Viareggio to have his picture taken. The picture was to be sent to Nino's father in America, so that he could see just how Nino looked and how much he had grown.

Viareggio was a real city. It had shops and street cars and a long promenade facing the sea, where people walked. Nino had heard a great deal about Viareggio, though he had never been there. One went there by boat, along the canal which began at "le Cappane," not very far from Grandfather's house. Nino had often walked as far as "le Cappane," but today was a very special occasion, and Signor Ditto was going to drive them to the canal in his donkey cart.

He arrived early, with Julio on the seat beside him. Julio wanted to go with Nino. He had never been to Viareggio. Couldn't he go along, just this one time?

"You never let me go any place," he complained. "It's always: 'Stay home,' or: 'You're not old enough.' I'm as old as Nino. Can't I go, Father?"

There was a lot of arguing about it. Signor Ditto waved his hands and rolled his eyes. Julio was stubborn. Grandfather said at last:

"Oh, let him come along, Ditto. He will be company for Nino."

Signor Ditto bit his knuckles, considered a moment, then

after crossing himself he took Julio by the arm. Pointing a warning finger at him, he said: "Well, remember now—no mischief!"

"Up we go," said Grandfather. He lifted Nino into the cart, and up went the covered wicker basket of food too.

"Keep your blouse and trousers clean, Nino," said his mother. "We want to show your father how nice you look in the photograph."

"Now, Mother, you know that Signor Ditto's cart is the cleanest in the village," Nino said.

It was true. Signor Ditto would far rather wear a soiled shirt than have people say that his cart was dirty. Whether he was hauling stone, grain, or the decayed lupine that is used for fertilizing the corn fields, his cart would be thoroughly scrubbed at the end of each day's work. It was the best-built and most beautifully decorated cart in the village.

Nino loved to ride in it. He liked the colored paintings on its deep sides; bright flowers in yellow, green, and crimson. There was a carving on each side, too, of a row of angels with interlaced wings all holding hands. Jacobo, who did such fine fresco painting on walls and ceilings, had made the pictures on Signor Ditto's cart.

Nino always fell in love with colored objects; he didn't like things that were too plain. One Sunday morning before going to mass he had even gone so far as to cut fancy scallops with Allinda's scissors all round the bottom edges of his trousers by way of decoration. Allinda had wept tears at the sight, but in the end she had had to laugh.

[61]

Now they were all ready to start. Julio had won the argument with his father and was as proud as a bantam rooster.

Nino felt very excited as the cart rumbled through the village street. There would be so many new things to see today. He loved seeing new things, and in everything that he saw he found beauty. The rustling of leaves was music to his ears. He always knew where flowers and berries grew the thickest, and when the chestnuts opened up their spiky burs, all lined with golden plush, to let the nuts fall. He loved birds and animals. He even liked hedgehogs, perhaps because they looked so like chestnut burs themselves, and he knew where they made their snug nests for the winter, burrowed deep under the earth and dead leaves. The hedgehogs were not afraid of him, but they did not like Julio. Julio always came home filled with prickles after a hedgehog hunt.

Julio had brought his mandolin today, and he played on it while they rode. He could already pick out quite a few simple tunes, and Nino knew the words to some of them. Just now he was singing the old folk song "O da Napoli a Torino" in a soft voice that carried above the rattling of the cart wheels. One by one, Grandfather, Signor Ditto, and Allinda took up the tune, and they all sang together. Even Caesar, sitting between Grandfather's knees, joined in with an occasional howl. The donkey's feet made sharp clicking sounds over the cobblestones as he trotted along.

The morning air was crisp. Parts of the village still slumbered in deep dark shadows. The sun was just rising beyond the monastery on the hilltop, above the Church of Santa

[62]

Lucia. The old building looked ghostlike, a misty violet against the coral sky. The hills were dark and clear, and Nino thought that everything had a holy look, like the pictures in church. He stopped his singing to gaze about him.

The cart jogged on towards the lowlands. The road wound about; it was longer coming this way than by the footpath that cut across the fields. They passed the Campo Santo, the old cemetery with its graves that dated back, some of them, to the twelfth century. Nino had seen the rows of old tombstones leaning against the wall. They had been taken up to make room for newcomers. Long ranks of black dusty cypress trees bordered the cemetery walls, and here and there a tall obelisk or a white cross reached above the wall and could be seen from the road outside.

[63]

"Do you remember the day we went to see the sexton dig up those old graves?" Nino asked.

"Yes," said Julio, shivering. "And he took us to look down that deep stone pit in the middle of the cemetery that was all full of bones. Ugh!"

"Just bones and bones," Nino said.

"Bones now," said Grandfather. "But in time they will all turn into thin dust."

"And by and by," Signor Ditto put in, "even that will become in turn a part of the earth. Who knows," went on the good Signor, who simply loved a discussion of this kind, "whose bones you might be stirring when you plow the fields!"

"We are nearly there now," said Allinda to the children.

The smell of the marshes reached their nostrils and they could see "le Cappane" a short distance ahead. Nino and Julio both craned their necks like young storks. They wished they were in the rowboat already.

Julio said aloud to himself: "I wish we were at 'le Cappane,' I wish we were in the boat, and I wish we were in Viareggio."

"If wishes were horses, beggars would ride," said Signor Ditto, who had a proverb for every occasion. Julio looked alarmed.

"Oh, Father, you'll let me go, won't you? You haven't changed your mind, have you?"

"No, Julio. My mind does not change like that, at every wind that blows. It is not a weathercock, like yours. I have

[64]

said you may go. Perhaps in the big city you may even buy a little sense for yourself."

Julio was so relieved that he threw his arms round his father's neck, almost dragging him off the seat. Signor Ditto, embarrassed by this affection, flushed a deep red, and without thinking gave the donkey a cut with the whip. With a startled jump the animal lurched forward. Signor Ditto and Grandfather tumbled backwards into the cart. Julio and Nino screamed.

Signor Ditto was the first to recover. Pulling on the reins, praying, coaxing, and pleading, he finally got the insulted donkey to slow down to his usual trot. Julio tried to hide in a corner of the cart. Signor Ditto hated to appear ridiculous, and was very apt to fly into a temper if anything happened to upset his dignity. He would certainly have made a scene now if Allinda, Grandfather, and Nino had not been laughing so hard that the poor man was unable to make himself heard. So in the end he gave in, and burst into laughter himself.

The cart passed under the shadow of the old stone building, and pulled up at the edge of the canal.

"Everybody out!" shouted Grandfather.

Caesar was the first. He made one leap over the side of the cart and ran round in circles, wagging his tail. The boys followed his lead and jumped to the ground. Allinda carried the wicker basket with the lunch while Grandfather went into the big stone barn to fetch the oars.

Signor Ditto said he would meet them here again a little after sundown and take them back to the village. He told

them all to have a good time in the big city. And to Grandfather he added confidentially:

"If my Julio doesn't behave himself, give him a good box
on the ear. Don't be afraid."

Grandfather smiled and said he would take care of Julio.

Signor Ditto drove back to the village, calling his donkey
endearing names. He still felt a little ashamed of that un-
fortunate whip cut.

The rest of the party settled themselves in the boat, which
had been tied under the willows. Grandfather spat on his
hands, dipped the oars into the water, and away they glided
down the long stretch of the canal. Water lilies floated on
the still surface, and the tall reeds near the shore rustled as
the boat moved along. Nino and Julio sat at the back and
dipped their hands into the water, now and then plucking a
blossom from among the flat round leaves. Once they surprised a little green frog basking in the center of a white
flower, but before they could catch him he went leaping
through the air and into the water.

They passed a canal boat. Two women with handkerchiefs on their heads walked on the bank, bending forward as they pulled the boat by long ropes fastened to their shoulders. A man stood at the prow of the boat, keeping it at a safe distance from the shore by means of a long pole. The man had a big scar on his cheek, and a black mustache. He was singing, to help the women keep time with their pulling. An eel swam by as they passed the canal boat, a huge black slimy one, wriggling just a few inches below the top of the water. Minnows darted like lightning, zigzagging now this way, now that, and green frogs hopped into the water from the grassy banks as the boat came near them.

"What a breakfast they would make!" said Julio. "Floured and fried, head, legs, and all. M-m!"

But Nino would far rather see them leaping into the water than in the pan.

The morning sun rose higher into the blue sky. Dragon-flies skimmed through the air like swallows. Julio tried to catch a bright blue one, but nearly fell into the water instead. Grandfather said that it was bad luck to catch a dragon-fly. He told them a story about a boy who once caught one and carried it in his pocket. The boy fell asleep in a corn field. When he woke up he found that all his fingers had been sewn tightly together with a fine silken thread.

"But who did it?" asked Nino and Julio both at once.

"Some say the dragon-fly escaped from the boy's pocket, and to get even with him sewed his fingers together. Others say that the dragon-fly had friends."

[67]

But he would not say who the dragon-fly's friends were. He only winked at Allinda, and went on rowing.

"Think of it!" said Julio. "Your fingers all sewed together like . . . like a shirt or a pair of pants or something!"

All this while the canal had been winding between fields of rice, fields of wheat and corn, with rows of tall poplars set at intervals along its banks. Now they were nearing Viareggio; Grandfather could tell by the group of thick willows in the distance. Caesar lay asleep near the lunch basket in the bottom of the boat.

"My stomach's flat," said Julio, wondering what the wicker basket contained.

Nino looked towards the city, and wished that he were already walking through its streets.

"Here we are," said Grandfather.

He looked for a good place under the huge willows, and made the boat fast to a limb. Caesar was the first out, as usual. He hurried around over the grass, sniffing in an interested way, and disappeared into a mass of tangled wild-rose bushes. He was gone for only a minute before he came back wagging his tail and bouncing about like a rubber ball.

Allinda spread the food out on a large white napkin on the grass: two loaves of bread thickly crusted, a small cheese, large red onions, and wine in a dark green bottle. There was salame, too, slices of smoked sausage, which Nino and Julio thought looked the best of all. Grandfather carelessly dropped a little paper bag into the middle of the cloth. Nino and Julio felt sure it must be a surprise for them.

[68]

"Here we have the staff of life," said Grandfather, breaking the loaves of bread and making the sign of the cross. "Its body is filled with millions of tiny cells that are filled with nature. When you put bread into your mouth, your mouth is filled with nature. It is filled with fire and water, the sky and the good earth. These are the four elements that give life to all things. Behold," Grandfather went on, dramatically, waving the hand that held the broken loaf, "behold the fire without warmth. Without it you could not bake this bread. And behold the water," he said, pointing to the canal. "Imagine water without fish; the sky without stars, without the moon and sun, and without birds. And then," he said, "think of the good earth, our kindly friend. Imagine the earth without trees, mountains, and rivers. Without all these, life

would perish. This bread is born of the elements. And this too is born of the elements," said Grandfather, and picking up a huge red onion, he peeled it carefully and sprinkled salt over it.

The old man ate the onion as if it had been an apple. He liked it better than salame. Salame always got into his teeth.

Julio held a piece of the hard salame in one hand and a chunk of cheese in the other, taking big mouthfuls of each in turn. Now and then he took a bite of bread to fill up what space might still be left in his mouth.

"I don't care so much for onions. They make me cry," said Nino. "But I do like salame and cheese!"

Allinda and Grandfather drank deeply from the dark green bottle. Sometimes the old man held the bottle a short distance in the air and let the red wine flow in a gurgling stream into his mouth. He rarely spilled a drop.

Julio told Nino that his father could do the same trick with a five-gallon demijohn. He had won a contest once at the village fair.

The little paper bag still lay untouched in the center of the napkin, and Julio leaned over to Nino and whispered in his ear: "I wonder what is in the bag."

Grandfather had guessed the secret between the two boys, and picking up the bag he opened it. Bright colored candy flew through the air and scattered on the green grass. The two boys hopped about like grasshoppers, picking up the sweets. Sometimes they made a leap for a candy that lay between them. Then two heads went crack. Grandfather and Allinda looked on in delight at the capering boys, who had found most of the treasure, but still went on looking.

Now and then a shout was heard: "Oh, I have found another!"

"Thank you," said Nino to his grandfather.

"Thank you," said Julio, his mouth bulging with candy. "Won't you have one?" he asked the old man, holding out a little round colored ball. "I think this one has a hazelnut in the middle."

The lunch was over and they made their way through the outskirts of the city. Nino and Julio were all eyes.

"Oh, look at that! Oh, look at this!" they kept calling out in their excitement.

They were soon on a street that led into Via della Pineta, a main thoroughfare lined with rows of tall slender cypresses that screened the sea from view. They could hear the waves splashing below them. The smell of the sea filled the air and the noon sun beat down warmly. There were many elegant shops on this street and the boys feasted their eyes to their hearts' content. They went through the marketplace, where crowds of people were buying and selling, some bargaining, some arguing at the top of their voices. Pigs squealed, chickens cackled, cows mooed, and an occasional bray from a stray donkey varied the chorus. Nino saw a man pull a stiletto from under his shirt to cut an apple with. He ate, holding the slice of apple and the weapon both in the same hand. Some day the man would take a slice off his nose doing that, thought Nino.

[71]

Carabinieri strolled through the crowd in spick and span uniforms of red, green, and gold, wearing black hats heaped with white plumes, and shining swords dangling at their sides. A street musician with an accordion was playing the national anthem. It made a lump come to Nino's throat.

"Oh, such music!" said Julio, fingering his mandolin.

Someone shouted to Julio: "*Musica, musica!*"

Julio felt embarrassed and his face turned quite red.

"Here's the place," said Grandfather at last. "See?" he said, pointing up to a carved sign over an arched doorway: "Giuseppe Magi, Photographer."

Nino read the sign after Grandfather: "Giuseppe Magi, Photographer."

Inside, the walls were covered with photographs, the work of many years. A little hunch-backed man, with a scraggling Vandyke beard and a nose like a strawberry, came forward.

"*Una bellissima giornata,*" said Grandfather to him.

"*Sì, sì, Signor,*" said the photographer, wiping his acid-stained hands on his trousers and then running his fingers through his bushy white hair, which stood almost on end.

Nino thought him very queer; his eyes were like those of a crow, deep and black, and the bushy white eyebrows above made his eyes look even blacker, like two little holes in his face.

"*Sì, Signor,* it is a beautiful day," said the little man. "But there's something in the air, sir. There certainly is. This morning when I got out of bed my old bones ached like a thousand sins. Either we are to have a storm, or my

[72]

old age is not true to me," said the photographer, shaking his head.

He turned to Allinda.

"Signora," he said. "Shall it be a picture of the bambinos or a group picture of all of you?"

Nino said: "Oh, Mother, we must have Caesar in the picture too! You know Father would like that."

While they waited for the photographer to prepare his camera the two boys looked at the numerous photographs that covered the walls. There were "oh's" and "ah's" as they moved from one to another. The pictures were of people in all walks of life. There were pictures of well-groomed and well-dressed gentlemen with fine flowing beards. Some had ribbons stretched across the front of their chests, with all kinds of medals hanging from them.

"This one looks like a duke," said Julio.

"He looks more like a mayor to me. See that double-pointed beard and the gold-headed cane?" said Nino. "Yes, he must be a mayor in full dress."

Another wall was covered with pictures of people in their wedding clothes. The shy brides simpered like dolls, while beside them the bridegrooms stood so stiffly and solemnly that they reminded Julio of pallbearers at a funeral. Nino, too, thought the bridegrooms' faces looked much too sad.

"Oh, look at the babies!" cried Nino presently.

There were little bambinos in swaddling-clothes, bambinos without even a stitch of clothing, and others in embroidered dresses, almost hidden under billows of lace and

[73]

ribbons and flounces. There were bambinos lying on their backs, others on their bellies; some crying, others laughing; some kicking up an awful fuss and others fast asleep.

There were little boys and girls in communion dresses, the girls all in white and the boys in black. There were soldiers in uniform, their legs crossed elegantly as they leaned against a marble pillar, holding their feathered hats in the crook of their elbow. The two boys liked the pictures of the hunters best of all: hunters in high leather boots and sheepskin coats, with rows of cartridges stuck in belts around their waists, holding a shotgun in one hand and a brace of dangling ducks or pheasants in the other.

"Oh, Nino," cried Julio, "look at this!"

Julio had found a photograph of a family group.

"Oh, my!" he said, and whistled a long low whistle. "What a lot of bread they must eat at one sitting! Think of it! Eighteen in all. What a big family!"

"Come," said Allinda to the two boys. "The Signor is ready now to take the picture."

Nino and Julio were both trying to count just how many boys and how many girls there were in the family group. This was difficult, as two in the group were tiny babies. So they had to give it up.

"Maybe they're girls, maybe they're boys," said Julio.

The photographer made Allinda sit in a huge carved chair, and Grandfather stood beside her with his right hand on her shoulder. Nino was placed on the other side, leaning with his elbow on his mother's lap. He stared into the

[74]

camera. Would the man never get through making arrangements? Nino thought his eyes would drop out of their sockets if he didn't blink them soon. The photographer rubbed his hands and surveyed the group with his black, beady little eyes.

He said: "Signor Nino, smile just a little. Do not look so pensive."

Julio, standing behind the photographer, was making faces by putting his two first fingers in his mouth and pulling outward. Nino laughed out loud.

"No, no," said the photographer. "Not so much smile! Just a little. Just a gentle one. It will make a beautiful picture." He pulled the black cloth over his head and the camera, like a tent. Nino could hear him fumbling about underneath it.

"All ready now," said the man. "Don't move. Smile."

A shout came from Julio.

"Why, you've forgotten to put Caesar in the picture!"

Grandfather called Caesar to his side. The dog came and sat beside his master, now and then looking up as if to ask: "What is all this fuss about?" He watched every movement, cocking his shaggy head first on one side, then on the other.

"All ready now," said the little man, popping out from under his cloth again.

He held a rubber ball in his right hand, while the left hand stuck out as if to give a signal.

"All ready. Quiet. Smile. Everybody smile now."

Even Julio, who was not in the picture, found himself smiling. Click, click, and it was all over. Nino was glad. He still felt as dazed as if he had been shot out of a cannon.

Once in the street again, the two boys begged to go down to the shore. On the way they passed a confectioner's shop and stopped, their eyes glued to the window. Grandfather led them in, and when everyone was seated at a round marble-topped table he called to the man behind the counter. "*Gelati per tutti!* Ice cream for everyone!"

It came in big slices. Julio took a first mouthful and cried out: "Oh, it makes my tongue ache!" Nevertheless he gobbled it down to the last frozen spoonful. Nino ate his slowly, trying to keep the different stripes of color even—red, white, and green—so that up to the very end it looked like a flag on his plate. They left the shop and walked toward the shore.

When they came in sight of the sea, Nino was spellbound.

[76]

Never had he imagined anything so beautiful as the blue water sparkling in the sun, the curled waves, each one different in shape and color, that broke and splashed on the shore.

They found an opening between the row of tall cypresses that led them down to the white sand. The west wind had blown the sand into little mounds.

"They look like waves, too," said Nino.

"Let's all go in wading," said Allinda, and before anyone else could speak the two boys were already in the water. Caesar was having a grand time barking at the waves. He chased them out as far as he could, then came running back. Sometimes the waves were a little too quick for him, and then he looked very surprised, shook his coat so as to send the water flying in a shower of drops, and then went through the whole performance all over again.

Nino and Julio stood and watched a steamer far out at sea. Sometimes the big waves hid it entirely from view. The sea was covered with white caps. There was a strong wind coming from the west, and the air tasted salt on their lips.

Allinda was gathering sea shells, while Grandfather sat on a little mound of sand looking out toward the passing steamer. Perhaps he was thinking about the many ports he had visited in days gone by, and how steamers had taken the place of the old sailing ships. Perhaps he even saw a change in the sea itself—who knows? After all, Grandfather was getting old. The sea breeze stirred the old man's white mustache as he sat on the mound and watched the young boys at play.

The salt water stung the boys' legs. Julio began to rub and scratch. "This isn't like the canal water," he said. "This water bites."

"Rub sand on it. Rub sand on it," said Nino, trying this singular cure himself. "That will stop the stinging."

Heavy gray clouds sailed across the blue sky. Nino looked up to watch their changing shapes. He always loved to see

[78]

the strange forms that clouds took: castles and animals, and sometimes even heads and faces; old men with long trailing beards or fat round-cheeked babies. The clouds sped overhead towards the east. To Nino it seemed as if the clouds themselves were standing still and it was really the earth that moved—the rocks, the sand, the row of tall cypresses, everything, turning faster and faster till he began to feel quite dizzy.

Time flew so quickly that the boys were not able to visit the museum or any of the buildings in the city. There was not even time to ride on the merry-go-round at the end of the promenade.

"It's too late," said Grandfather, looking at the sun. "We shall have to hurry now, to get back to 'le Cappane' before it gets too dark along the canal."

To Nino it seemed like years since he had left the village. He was glad now that they were on their way home. Julio would rather have stayed in Viareggio a little longer. As they walked along he lagged behind, carrying his mandolin and the pocketful of sea shells Allinda had picked up for him. He looked here and there, afraid of missing some important sight in the big city.

They reached the canal and Grandfather unfastened the boat. Then beneath the long shadows of the willows they started homeward.

"The clouds are beautiful today," Nino said to his mother. "Look! See how the color changes when the sun shines through them."

[79]

Julio had been listening while Nino talked about the clouds and how beautiful they looked, but, strain his eyes as he might, he could see nothing more than just plain clouds. It was true that the clouds moved, but what was all this beauty that Nino was always talking about? Once when Jacobo came to tint the walls of the big room in their house, Julio had heard him speak of beauty to his father.

He had heard Jacobo say: "Signor Ditto, even a plain wall can be a beautiful thing."

To Julio it was still just a wall. He couldn't see what Nino saw in clouds anyway. They were just clouds. To Julio, they came and went, that was all. Julio played on his mandolin.

"It's not half as long going back as it was coming," he said.

He looked towards the distant hills and the village of Massarosa. Grandfather rowed on, but every once in a while he lifted his face anxiously to the sky.

CHAPTER V

VOICES IN THE NIGHT

STORMS come up quickly over the lowlands. The clouds that Nino thought so beautiful had gathered closer now. They looked spiteful and threatening. The sky darkened to an inky black and a muffled roll of thunder rumbled in the distance.

"*Pare il diluvio*," said Grandfather, looking up.

And it did look as if a deluge were at hand. All at once lightning ripped the heavens, slashing through the clouds and turning the black to a violet gray. There was a sharp clap of thunder, this time near by.

"If there's a deluge," said Julio cheerfully, "we shall be drowned like rats!"

[81]

"This is no time for joking," said Grandfather, and he pulled on the oars more quickly, with short even strokes.

The boat sped through the water with sudden jerks. Nino watched the sky, fascinated by the flashes of lightning. The wind that had risen all in a moment moaned and swept over the marshes, whipping the tall grass with rustling sounds. The tall poplars bent as though turning their backs to its fury; they looked like black giants in the night. It began to rain, big drops that glistened like pearls as they fell, and the surface of the canal, so still a moment ago, broke into a thousand dancing bubbles.

The rain pelted them without mercy. At the first heavy downfall Caesar had snuggled under the seat at the back of the boat.

"There's a light at 'le Cappane'!" cried Julio, peering through the darkness.

"Signor Ditto is waiting for us," Grandfather said. "I hope he has a fire started."

They reached the shore soaked to the skin. "We're like drowned rats!" cried the irrepressible Julio. "That's what we are—we're like drowned rats!"

It was raining in torrents now. In the doorway of "le Cappane" Signor Ditto stood holding a lantern and shouting: "*Caminate presto!* Hurry up!" at the top of his voice.

To Nino the voice sounded miles and miles away.

"Looks to me as if the end of the world was coming," said Signor Ditto as the four rushed through the open doorway of the barn.

Julio stood for a moment, staring in consternation. All at once he turned. made a dash for the door again, and disappeared into the night. He had suddenly remembered his precious mandolin, left in the boat.

Signor Ditto shouted to him to come back.

"O testa di una capra!" he cried, running after Julio. "Come back, come back, you goat-headed good-for-nothing!"

Stubborn as a goat, indeed, Julio stumbled on through the darkness, deaf to all cries. He reached the boat, found his beloved mandolin, and turned to plunge back again to shelter. Dashing headlong, he ran straight into Signor Ditto, who was still groping and muttering on his track. There was a violent collision; father and son sat down abruptly in puddles of water. Signor Ditto, furious, called loudly on every saint in the calendar, and he wasn't blessing them, either. Julio rubbed his smarting head. After all, he'd only gone to fetch his mandolin. He didn't see why his father should get so fussed up about a little thing like that!

But, once in the dim candlelight of the huge barn, he was overwhelmed with tragedy and he burst into tears.

Signor Ditto, still angry, shouted in a sarcastic voice: "And now what's the matter with my little bag of honey?"

But Julio for once was speechless. Silently he held out the broken mandolin, dangling by its strings. The pride and joy of his soul had been crushed in that unlucky fall. It was tragic, it was terrible, a wreck past all mending. A thousand times rather would Julio have broken his own stubborn head.

[83]

But to the others, sorry as they were for Julio, there was still something comic in the scene—the shouting and excitement, the ridiculous sight of father and son sitting splash in the puddle, Signor Ditto's fury, and now this unexpected tragic ending. In spite of themselves they began to laugh.

But Julio was beside himself. "You'll have to get me another one!" he yelled, suddenly recovering his voice. "L-look at it! You'll just have to get me another!"

Poor Signor Ditto was about at the end of his tether. He made the sign of the cross, chewed his knuckles, and cast his eyes to the ceiling.

"*O Dio, O Dio, che miseria!* God, what a life of misery!"

Little by little he calmed down. Allinda tried to console Julio, who still gulped and sniffled. Gradually peace was restored, and they all gathered round the fire to dry their clothes. Outside, the storm still raged. Shutters were banging upstairs and the wind whistled in the big chimney.

"Will this turmoil ever come to an end!" demanded Signor Ditto, twisting round to scrape the mud from the seat of his trousers as he stood before the crackling fire.

"I only hope the wind won't blow the tiles off from over our heads. Do you remember," said Grandfather, "what it did to the roof of the olive mill year before last?"

"Indeed I do! There wasn't a whole tile left."

Nino thought of the rakka box story Grandfather had told him, and huddled nearer to his mother. Suppose this roof did blow off?

Julio said: "I'm hungry again. Oh, but I'm hungry!"

[84]

Signor Ditto turned on him. "What? Again? All you think of is your miserable stomach!"

Allinda, the peace maker, began to search in the basket.

"There's still some bread and cheese, and a bit of salame," she said. "It isn't much, but we can share it."

The donkey, unhitched from his harness, was eating hay from a huge pile stacked in one corner of the barn. Nino could hear the steady, comfortable grinding of his teeth as he chewed. It made him hungry just to listen to it.

They divided the remains of food from the basket. Julio said: "I'm *still* hungry."

His father fairly glowered at him.

"For once, Julio, you can't have what you want."

"I know what we'll do," said Allinda.

Everyone looked at her as though she were possessed of magic powers. Allinda smiled. She got up from the box she was sitting on and said: "At least I can appease Julio's hunger. I'm not so sure about the rest of you."

She crossed the wide floor, to where on one wall were hanging the long strings of white and yellow corn, left there to dry out for seed. Sorting out some of the biggest ears, she brought them over to the fire, giving one to each of the boys. Julio looked at his grumpily.

"I can't eat that. What do you think I am—a rooster?"

"Popcorn, popcorn," said Allinda, and added, smiling: "You'd like that, Julio, wouldn't you?"

"Popcorn!" shouted the boys. "That'll be fun!"

"Oh, Allinda," said Julio, suddenly repentant, "you do

[85]

think of everything." He gave her a tight squeeze, sorry now for his rudeness.

"Now, Nino, you take this knife and see how many kernels you can dig out."

Working away like two squirrels by the fireside, the boys soon had a good-sized heap on the floor. Julio dug his teeth into the dry cob and took the kernels out that way.

Grandfather and Signor Ditto sat and smoked. Outside, the storm still raged.

Allinda took a couple of the large iron sieves used to separate the chaff from the grain, and putting the hulled corn into one she placed the other sieve over it and tied the two together with wire. She hung the sieves over the fire and shook them back and forth with a long iron poker. Nino and Julio watched. Soon the kernels began to pop.

"It is good of you, Mother," said Nino. "I'd never have thought of it, especially on a night like this. No one will ever starve while you're around."

Grandfather said: "You'll learn, Nino, as you grow. You'll learn lots of things you don't know now."

Julio said: "If we had some chestnuts, they'd taste better than popcorn."

Grandfather went to the basket and fumbled in it till he found a little twisted paper of salt. He said to the boys: "Here, try some of this on it."

The popcorn tasted much better with salt.

"Hoo, hoo, hoo!" came a hollow voice from somewhere in the room. "Hoo, hoo!"

[86]

The two boys stood as if frozen to the floor. Julio's eyes rolled in terror. Nino, his mouth still full of popcorn, stared about the room.

"It can't be the donkey," he thought. "Donkeys don't make hoo, hoo noises. It must be an owl." But all the same he could feel his heart beginning to thump.

The voice came again: "Hoo, hoo!"

"It's ghosts, it's ghosts! The place is haunted!" shouted Julio, jumping to his feet. "Let's get out of here, quick. I'd rather be soaked to the skin than stay here with a ghost!" He looked positively scared.

"Julio, calm yourself. There's nothing to be afraid of,"

[87]

said Signor Ditto, who wasn't any too sure himself what that queer noise was.

Nino said: "It's only an owl."

But Julio persisted, his eyes as big as saucers. "It's a ghost, I tell you!"

"It is not!"

"It is so."

"It isn't."

"I tell you it is. There! There it is again," cried Julio, frantic now with terror.

He stood shivering in the firelight, rolling his eyes. Just at that moment the donkey over in the corner cleared his throat and gave a deep gusty cough. It was the last blow. Julio went into tantrums, stamping his feet and shouting: "I want to go home! I want to go home!"

He had forgotten his hunger. He didn't care about eating any more. All he wanted was to be safe at home in his own bed.

Nino said: "Don't be so scared, Julio; it's only an owl. You'll see in the morning. We'll look for it. It must be up in the rafters somewhere."

He went round the room, gazing up into the big rafters that supported the floor above. At all cost he wanted to prove to Julio that it was only an owl that had made the noise. But peer as he might, he could see nothing. No more sounds from the ghost were heard, however, and at last Julio said hopefully: "Maybe it was just passing by."

But still every time the wind made a shutter bang, or the

[88]

donkey shuffled or even cleared his throat, Julio was uneasy.

Impossible to go home tonight. They would have to sleep here in the barn. Allinda began carrying armfuls of hay to a corner near the fireplace, and Nino helped her, patting the hay down to make a smooth, even bed.

"What fun this is!" he said. "I always wanted to sleep in hay."

Julio carried armfuls of hay too, but not without casting an uneasy glance over his shoulder every moment towards the dim corners of the room. He said: "Father, do you think Mother will be worried about us?"

"Not if it's raining as hard at home as it is here."

The two boys bounced up and down on the hay till the dust flew, and Grandfather began sneezing. Nino said: "God bless you!"

Soon they were all lying snug. Only their heads stuck out of the hay. Julio, next to his father, went right to sleep. Nino lay awake watching the firelight playing on the huge oaken rafters above his head. Sleeping in hay wasn't quite so easy as he had thought; it tickled his nose and stuck into his neck, every time that he moved. In the occasional lull of the wind he could hear the heavy breathing of the donkey, drowsing in his corner. As the fire burned low, Nino's eyes grew more used to the darkness. Everyone but him was fast asleep. Presently he got up softly and threw another piece of wood on the fire.

His mother stirred, and said in a sleepy voice: "Nino, what are you doing? Be quiet. You'll wake Julio."

Nino lay awake thinking of many things. Now and then Signor Ditto snored, a snore that ended with a funny little whistling sound. The more Nino tried to sleep, the wider awake he got. What was the use of just lying here in the hay? he thought. Things were going on outside. Would he dare steal upstairs? he asked himself. Could he do it without waking the others? He moved slowly—ever so slowly. The hay rustled, but only a little. Now he stood in his bare feet on the floor. Very carefully he pulled on his shoes. The firelight threw his shadow across the walls, a shadow ten times, twenty times bigger than Nino.

"I'm not afraid of the dark," he said to himself.

He crept softly towards the stairs that led up to the loft. Once up in that huge bare space, Nino felt a little scary. He went to a window facing the marshes and the canal. The wind had died down by now; he could see the black clouds parting to let a star or two peer through. The marshes lay in dense blackness; mournful it was. Only the water in the canal winding through the marshes shone a pale gray in the night.

From below, Nino could still hear Signor Ditto snoring. He knew it was he by the little whistle at the end of each snore. The sound kept him from feeling lonely, up here by himself. It came softly up the stairs and into the loft.

He walked about carefully. He found another window opposite, which faced the village. Through it he could just make out the black outline of the hills against the sky. A few lights twinkled in the village. Presently he saw a faint gray light among the clouds; the moon was coming out. The light

grew stronger, turning to a silvery color as the moon slid slowly into sight. Now he could see the hills and the village; he could see even Casa Checchi, high up on the slope.

For a long time Nino stood there, peering out. As it grew lighter and lighter outside, his eyelids grew heavier and heavier, but still he could not drag himself away. More stars shone in the sky, and the wind had calmed down almost to a silence.

Nino thought: I'd better go back now.

Yet something held him there, gazing out. It must be nearly morning, he thought. He went back to the other

[9 1]

window, facing the marshes. A faint light was rising in the east; the flat horizon was just visible.

Oh, I can't go back to sleep now, Nino thought.

He felt cheered at the sight of day breaking. He waited, looking out over the marshes while the others slept. If Mother finds out, she'll be angry, he thought, but still he didn't move. He saw the sky patterned with tiny coral clouds. The marshes took on a fresher green, and the canal sparkled silvery gray through the mist. A flock of ducks flew over the marshes, keeping a low steady course. Nino felt as if he had grown, grown older, standing there by the window. He felt as though a long time had passed by, and he had been in the loft for years. Suddenly he was startled by his mother's voice, calling from the room below.

"Nino, Nino, where are you?"

She sounded vexed and startled. Nino ran to the stairhead.

"Mother, come! Come quickly. The sun is rising. Hurry or you'll miss it." Running down, he called again: "Come quick, Mother. It's going to be the most lovely sunrise you ever saw." And he dashed back again to his window.

Allinda shook the hay from her dress and hair.

"I wonder if that boy has been up all night," she said to Grandfather, who was awake too. Julio and his father were still fast asleep.

Grandfather smiled.

"Let him see the sunrise, Allinda. It's good to see the sun rise after such a storm as last night."

Allinda stood beside Nino. The sun was just coming over

[92]

the horizon. The coral-lined clouds changed slowly to pink, then to orange and rose. Like a ball of fire the sun came up over the rim of the marshes. It seemed to spin red-hot, and the marshes were transformed into lavender and the mist into silver.

"I told you it was going to be the most beautiful sunrise you ever saw," Nino said.

Mother and child stood by the window and watched the making of another day.

"You are right," said Allinda. "It is the most beautiful sunrise I have ever seen."

She stooped and gave her son a good-morning kiss on the forehead. They went downstairs, and found Grandfather throwing fagots on the fire. Julio and Signor Ditto never stirred. They lay half buried in the straw. The donkey was pulling huge mouthfuls of hay from the stack. Grandfather pulled Julio by the leg and said: "Wake up. It's time for breakfast."

Julio woke with a start and began to rub his eyes.

"I'm so hungry! What is there for breakfast this morning, Mother?"

Nino laughed, and Grandfather and Allinda fairly roared.

"Popcorn!" they cried.

The sleepy Julio came to his senses at this, and in turn woke his father.

"Let's go home, Father. The storm is over now," he said.

"You missed the most beautiful sunrise this morning, Julio," Nino told him. "Never, never will you see one like

Mother and I saw. I only wish I had thought of waking you."

"Why didn't you? We could have been half-way home by now. I'm so hungry," Julio added, picking up some stray grains of popcorn from the floor. "I do hope Mother has lots and lots of polenta with cheese!"

Signor Ditto had a hard time dragging the donkey away from the hay, but after much coaxing he got him hitched up to the cart. They jogged along the road towards the village. The morning sun threw long shadows on the muddy road. Birds sang in the clear morning air. They drove into the courtyard, and Signora Ditto came out, shading her eyes with her hand.

"I'm so glad you're all safe," she said. "I didn't sleep a wink last night for fear something had happened to you all."

"We had a wonderful time, Mother," said Julio. "Didn't we, Nino? Popcorn, hay, ghosts—and the trip to Viareggio was wonderful. Oh, but I broke my mandolin."

"Come in and tell me all about it," said the fat Signora. "You must be famished, missing two meals."

Julio darted into the house. Nino followed him. Breakfast was all ready; heaps of fried polenta with goat cheese.

"It's a good thing we didn't come back last night," said Julio, his mouth full. "There wouldn't have been half as much left to eat this morning!"

CHAPTER VI

THE PROCESSION

JUST above the village was a hill called Tre Croci, or the
Hill of the Three Crosses. Right on top of it was a tiny
chapel, where once a year the priest said mass. Very early
on that morning, almost before daybreak, everyone gathered
in the village square before the church steps, and from there

the procession started, led by the priest in his robes, along the village street and up the steep winding path that led to Tre Croci.

This year Nino was to be one of the boys who walked in the procession, carrying candles. It was the first year he had been old enough to take part in the procession with the others and he felt it to be a great event. For days he had talked of nothing else.

Allinda was up early that morning, cleaning Nino's shoes. Sitting by the fire she warmed a piece of thick bacon rind before the flame, rubbed the shoes with it thoroughly, and then polished them with a woolen cloth. The leather shone brightly in the firelight.

"Look, Nino," she said. "Your shoes look as good as new."

Nino sat on a stool, his bare feet towards the fire. He was wearing a new black smock with a white collar and cuffs, and his hair was very smoothly slicked and parted.

"I'm so glad I can go!" he said to his mother when the shoes had been laced on. "Even though I'm the youngest of the boys, I'll do my best."

Allinda replied: "Of course you will, but you mustn't forget that it's a long climb, Nino."

"If the others can do it, I can," Nino said proudly.

He wriggled his toes inside the shoes, which were stout and heavy, and a little bit tight. Nino's feet were growing so fast that now there was very little room for his toes. They were his best shoes, and as he wore them so seldom he had already begun to outgrow them. But they looked very nice.

Nino and his mother walked to the square facing the church. A crowd of boys dressed in black and white stood about whispering. The priest was passing candles to some, crucifixes to others, and banners to the oldest ones.

Nino took the long candle the priest handed to him and held it tightly in his hand. He whispered to Allinda: "Look, Mother, the sun is rising. We'll start soon."

Golden shafts shot upward fanlike into the sky above the gray church, piercing the mist that still hung over the hills. A few stars twinkled faintly in the west. The sun rose majestically over the dome of the church. Nino watched it stand, a great red ball, directly behind the cross on the dome, so that the arms of the cross seemed to split it into four parts. The cross stood out black against the round fiery background.

"Isn't it a glorious sight?" said Nino to his mother, who, kneeling by his side, was making sure that the laces on Nino's shoes were securely fastened.

"Yes, it is, Nino. Just gorgeous for such a day as this."

In single file the procession made its way along the narrow path through the hills, led by the priest who was carrying a huge cross with an image of the Saviour on it. Mothers and fathers walked along beside their children. Nino held the lighted candle with both hands in front of him. He could smell the wax as he walked carefully along the path.

They came to the first shrine along the path, a small weatherbeaten gray structure. It housed the Virgin Mary. The figure stood holding the babe in her arms; the red in her robe had turned to a sienna, and her face was a faded gray. The procession formed a semicircle around the shrine and knelt in prayer.

Slowly they moved on, with pauses at each shrine. In the open air the candles flickered palely; where the path wound through woods, overhung by the trees, they shone out strong and clear like candles in a church. The smell of burning wax hung warm on the air.

They had reached the eighth shrine, when Nino complained to his mother.

"Mother, my shoes. My shoes are too tight. They hurt my feet. I wish I could take them off. May I, Mother?" Nino whispered. "I think I could walk better in my bare feet."

"We will soon be there, Nino. Be brave," Allinda said.

The wax from the candle trickled down and fell on Nino's hands. It stung for a moment, then hardened. He kept scraping at it from time to time with his finger nails.

"Be cheerful, Nino," said his mother. "There are only six more shrines, and then we can rest at the top of the hill."

Nino knew there were fourteen shrines along the way to the top, representing the fourteen stations of the cross. He saw Julio up toward the front of the procession, and wondered if Julio's shoes hurt his feet, too.

The eighth and ninth shrines were passed, and when Nino reached the tenth his eyes were filled with tears, his hands were covered with wax, and his feet felt like hot coals.

Nino said: "I've got to take them off."

He handed the candle to his mother, who held it in one hand and with the other helped to unlace his shoes.

"Oh!" said Nino, feeling an immense relief. He wondered how he could have stood those tight shoes so long.

Some of the other boys looked longingly at Nino. They too would have liked to do the same thing, but didn't dare. Nino walked barefooted to the twelfth shrine, but he felt no better. The sharp stones on the path cut into the soles of his feet. His mother walked patiently by his side.

"Only two more shrines," she whispered.

The boys overheard "two more shrines" and heaved deep sighs of relief. By the time the procession reached the fourteenth shrine, the group was feeling more dead than alive. They knelt once more. In this shrine the Saviour was nailed

to the cross. There were red trickles of painted blood on His
hands and feet, and the sight made Nino feel ashamed of his
own weakness.

By the time the procession reached its goal, the banners
lay slantwise, and many of the candles had burned out. The
boys sat down on the bare ground and after taking off their
shoes rubbed the soles of their feet.

"Thank goodness! We're at the top," said Nino. But his
bare feet still ached and burned.

His mother took a cloth, poured some water on it from a
bottle which she had brought with her, and bathed his feet.

"That was the longest three miles I ever walked," said Julio, as he came over and sat down beside Nino. Julio was on his own today, and felt very proud of the fact.

"Hush up, Julio," said Nino. "The priest might hear you."

It was very still up here on the hilltop. It seemed like being on the top of the world, Nino thought. In the valley below he could see the village. The sun glittered on the golden dome of the church. The houses looked tiny and far away.

On this space of level ground that topped the hill three huge crosses towered. They could be seen for miles around. Nino had seen them often from the village and it gave him a strange feeling now to be so close to them. They looked immense. The chapel that stood before the middle cross was quite tiny, not much bigger than a shrine. When the door was opened, there was just enough room for the priest to stand before the little altar; the boy who served mass had to kneel on the step outside, and all the people knelt in a circle on the grass around. Olive trees surrounded the open space like an amphitheater.

The priest's voice sounded muffled and solemn inside the chapel. Three times the little bell tinkled, sharp and clear on the still air and all the people bowed their heads. Then, standing before the chapel, the priest told the story of the birth and death of the Lord. He quoted from the gospel according to Saint Matthew, and it seemed to Nino that the sermon lasted an hour. Many of the boys began to fidget. Nino's feet felt better, but he was beginning to get very hungry. He was glad when the sermon was over.

Everyone sat round on the grass and ate from the baskets and bags which the fathers and mothers had brought along. The priest sat surrounded by heaps of crosses, banners, and burned-out candles. He was eating too. To Julio, who had been waiting impatiently, this breakfast was the best part of the whole procession.

After breakfast the groups disbanded. Some went down the path back to the village, with the priest; others strolled about the hillside. Wild flowers—pink, red, yellow, and blue—covered the slopes beneath the olive trees. Nino picked several big bunches of violets, and Allinda wrapped the flowers in a wet cloth and put them in her basket.

"We'll make a wreath for Grandfather," she said. "You know it is his birthday today."

Nino had not forgotten. "We'll make him a big wreath," he said. "I'll pick a lot more flowers, blue lupines and dandelions, and we can put them among the violets."

Already he could see how lovely the wreath would look.

On their way down the path Allinda stopped to gather fagots while Nino, at the edge of a little brook, picked rich green ferns to add to the wreath. There was moss too, velvet-smooth, and leaves of wild parsley. The basket was soon filled.

"Mother, just smell them. The violets smell the best," said Nino, bending his face over the basket as he sprinkled water to keep the flowers fresh.

Julio searched about for chestnuts among the green chestnut leaves.

"They won't be ripe before October," Nino told him.

"I know," said Julio. "I was looking for last year's nuts. Sometimes the bur doesn't open. You can often find good chestnuts the year after."

After climbing many trees Julio came back without any chestnuts, his knees all the worse for his efforts.

Nino heard voices along the path. People going back to the village, he thought. He heard some of the boys rambling down the path, making a great din and breaking branches as they went, shouting and dragging their banners behind them.

Julio, who despite his scratched knees, had not given up his tree-climbing, dropped to the ground beside him and shouted: "Look, Nino! Robin's eggs!" He held two tiny pale blue eggs in the palm of his hand.

"They're beautiful, Julio, but you ought to put them back. The mother robin will be worried about them. Put them back where you found them, please," said Nino.

Julio hemmed and hawed, but finally he walked back to the tree with Nino and, climbing high up, put the eggs back in the nest. There was a fluttering and chirping overhead. Nino could see the mother robin frantically chattering about and beating her wings.

"Julio, you shouldn't have done that," said Nino. "How are we going to have robins if you take their eggs?"

"Let's be on our way," said Allinda to the boys.

She lifted three bundles of neatly tied fagots to her head. Nino and Julio carried the basket between them while Allinda walked ahead, stopping now and then to clear a branch that hung over the path. Soon they were home. Nino and his mother made their way through the courtyard towards the house. Grandfather was nowhere to be seen.

"Aren't we lucky!" said Nino, after searching the house to make sure that he was not around. "Now we can make the wreath without his knowing all about it beforehand. Won't he be surprised? I'll get the string, Mother. Where are the scissors?"

"You'll find them on the shelf above the loom," she said, throwing down the bundle of fagots in the corner by the fireplace.

Mother and son bent over the fascinating task of making the wreath. The flowers and ferns were intertwined and tied, and when it was all done the wreath looked beautiful, as Nino knew it would.

"A florist could not have made a better one," he said. "Best of all, it doesn't look a bit like a funeral wreath."

[105]

"It might have," said his mother, "if we had put more blue in it."

They hung it on the wall over Grandfather's chair in the corner, by the window that faced the yard.

"Hello, Nino. Did you enjoy the procession?" Grandfather asked as he entered the house.

"Oh, it was wonderful!" said Nino. "It was wonderful!"

He had already forgotten all about his tight shoes, but Allinda said: "His feet troubled him badly going up the path. He's outgrown his shoes."

"I'll see the cobbler and we'll have a new pair made for you," Grandfather said.

Nino waited for Grandfather to go and sit in the big chair, but instead Grandfather walked about the room, not going anywhere near it.

"Will he ever go and sit down?" whispered Nino to his mother.

At last Nino said: "Grandfather, you must be tired. Won't you sit down?"

"Not a bit tired," said the old man cheerfully. "Have to feed the pigs and chickens now." And he disappeared out the door.

Nino stood looking at the wreath, quite disappointed.

His mother said: "You're too impatient. Wait, he'll see it when he comes in. He always sits in his favorite chair after feeding the stock. You know that. Your grandfather couldn't smoke his pipe without that chair!"

Grandfather came back, sat in the chair, and took out his

[106]

pipe. Nino watched anxiously from the corner of his eye.

"Smells grand. What is it?" Grandfather turned his head about him and sniffed the air. "Bless my soul!" he said, looking up at the wreath. "Bless my soul! What a beau-ti-ful wreath!" he said, drawing out the "beautiful."

"Do you like it?" said Nino, all excitement. "Mother and I made it specially for you."

Allinda said: "Happy birthday, Father."

Nino, too, wished his grandfather a happy birthday. Grandfather looked surprised, scratched his head, and then gave his daughter an affectionate hug.

He said: "Allinda, I don't know what I'd do without you and Nino."

"That isn't all, Father."

She took a bright red scarf out from under a pile of woven materials that stood heaped up on the frame of the loom.

[107]

"Happy birthday again," she said, putting the red scarf around her father's neck.

"Oh, thank you, Allinda! Just what I needed," said the old man, looking at the ends of the scarf.

Allinda had woven two roosters, one on each end.

Nino said: "Cock-a-doodle-do. How old are you?"

Grandfather laughed. "I don't remember. Let me see!"

He turned the woolen scarf over and over in his hands thoughtfully.

"How old am I? How old am I, Allinda?" he asked jokingly. "I'm so old I've forgotten my age," he said to Nino, still laughing.

"How old are you?" Nino persisted. "How old are you today?"

"Let me see," said the old man. "I was born in April 1843. It is now April 1905. How old does that make me?" he said to Nino. "Let me see you figure that out."

Nino counted on his fingers, and gave up. Several times he tried and gave up, and started all over again. At last, going to the fireplace, he picked up a piece of charcoal. After considerable struggling he arrived at the figure sixty-two. He was so sure of this figure that he stopped long enough to draw a rooster on the hearth with what was left of the charcoal. Then he sprang up and said proudly: "Cock-a-doodle-do. You're just sixty-two. You're just sixty-two."

"Good boy!" said Grandfather. "Your arithmetic is improving."

Grandfather stood looking at the wreath and at the scarf.

"It is a beautiful wreath, Nino," he said again, and he gave Nino a kiss on the forehead.

"It is a beautiful scarf, Allinda," he said to his daughter, and the old man gave Allinda a kiss on her forehead too. Then he sat down in his favorite chair and lit his pipe, still fingering the scarf while he smoked.

Nino went to the garden below the terrace to pick some parsley. His mother was going to fry frogs that night. She always sprinkled parsley and garlic over them to make them taste better.

Allinda was frying frittelle, too, in a skillet over the fire.

"How do you make frittelle?" said Nino to his mother. "They smell good."

"Beat two eggs well, put in two coffee spoons of sugar, one soup spoon of lard, and a pinch of salt. Mix well, stir, then add flour until you get a thick batter like dough; roll it out with a roller and flour it well. Then cut it in squares and fry it in half olive oil and half lard."

The pancakes sputtered and crackled in the skillet. Allinda sprinkled sugar on them after they were cooked. Nino liked frittelle that way.

[109]

After their meal Nino sat by the fire drawing on some pieces of paper that Jacobo had given him. Working in silence, he tried to make a picture of the procession. With a piece of charcoal held firmly in his hand, Nino drew the procession, starting with the priest carrying the cross at the front, right down to himself barefooted at the end. He put in even his mother, carrying his shoes.

"Oh!" shouted Nino. "If I only had colors! If I only had some green and yellow and red and blue. If I only had some colors," he went on, "I could make a really true procession."

Allinda and Grandfather looked over his shoulder, amazed at what he had done in such a short time.

"Look, Allinda," said Grandfather. "That really does look like Father Bellarosa. See him carrying the cross, and look at his bald head!"

Allinda looked closer. "And see, Father! He has put me in the picture, too. Oh, Nino," she said, "it's just like a real procession!"

Nino dashed off three crosses on the mount above the procession.

"There," he said. "It's almost finished now."

He knelt awhile, thinking and studying what he had done, while Allinda looked on. "I feel so good inside," he said to her.

He put in a few birds flying through the air, and last of all a blazing sun directly over the middle cross on the mountain top.

"There!" he said, getting up. "That finishes the picture."

CHAPTER VII

EASTER

THERE was much excitement at Casa Checchi as Easter Sunday drew near. The courtyard was swept clean and the house scrubbed from ceiling to floor. Everything had to be in perfect order for the many guests who were expected. They would eat at a long table in the courtyard. In preparation for the occasion, the oven had been kept hot for several days.

Allinda had made huge piles of small cakes sprinkled with red, yellow, and pale blue sugar crystals; also there was panettone, a large cake filled with pine nuts, raisins, and chopped angelica. For the children she had baked little soldiers and roosters of cake dough glazed with a mixture of beaten eggs and sugar. Raisins were used for the buttons and eyes. They came from the oven slick and shining. Long lines of chocolate cookies lay on the table. Some were shaped like stars; others like half-moons and crescents; and still others took the form of balls. Next to the cookies lay the huge round sweet bread generously sprinkled through with aniseed and looking like a giant doughnut. Last of all, Allinda made the sweet green squash tarts sprinkled with cinnamon and sugar. These were immense and looked like cart wheels before they were cut into small pieces.

Nino seldom left his mother's side these days.

"Oh, let me braid the fancy loaves!" he would beg, or: "May I beat the eggs?" or: "I want to sprinkle the colored sugar, Mother. You know how I like doing that."

Allinda worked tirelessly, calling on her son from time to time. "Nino, bring me the big wooden spoon. Nino, wash this bowl," and more often: "Nino, get out from under my feet!"

Nino knew what fun Easter could be, with all the guests and the big table set out in the open air of the courtyard.

"Easter doesn't last long enough. It's like Christmas—it comes and goes too quickly," he said to himself.

At last Easter Sunday came, and Nino, looking out of his open window, saw a cloudless sky deep emerald in color. The song of the birds sounded sweeter than usual, and, in the distance, he could hear the voices of peasants singing in the clear morning air. He jumped from his bed and dressed quickly in the clean clothes his mother had laid out for him. Today would be too full to waste any part of it. While he was washing, he could hear Grandfather and one of the neighbors in the courtyard. They were busy setting up the long table which soon would groan with the weight of the holiday meal.

The morning sun climbed higher into the sky while Nino and Grandfather walked to church to attend Easter mass. As they walked along, Nino heard the bells ringing. Allinda, who had gone to the early mass, stayed at home to get ready for the guests, who would appear directly after the second mass was over.

Nino and Grandfather entered the church. They touched their fingers to the holy water at the font and made the sign of the cross. The mass had just started and the organ was playing in deep melodious tones. Today the altar decorations were even finer than usual. There were more lighted candles and many more flowers. There were more altar boys today, too, and the choir sounded louder than it did on other days.

"I would like to be an altar boy," Nino whispered to his grandfather, kneeling beside him on the small bench.

"Perhaps some day you may be," replied the old man quietly.

There was more kneeling than on other days, thought Nino, as he shifted his weight from one knee to the other. Glancing about, he noticed that some people knelt on only

one knee. He tried this position too, but found it made little difference. His knees ached just the same.

"Be still, Nino," cautioned Grandfather.

The priest had just finished drinking from the sacred chalice and setting it down covered it with a spotless white napkin. He chanted the service in low sonorous tones. Two small altar boys held up the train of his sumptuous robe, which was covered with gold embroidery. It had a blue cross on the front and one on the back. Nino craned his neck to see him better. A boy kept changing the huge missal, a large book, from one side of the altar to the other. Another rang a little bell between the chants. The priest turned, bowed, and turned again with his back to the congregation. He bowed again. The smallest of all the altar boys ran back and forth with two small bottles of water and wine. He poured a little of each into the large silver and gold chalice that the priest held firmly in both hands. The priest blessed the congregation, blessed himself, and then with both hands lifted the large chalice to his mouth and drained it to the last drop. The organ played a triumphant strain, and the voices of the choir rang out, almost drowning the priest's words.

Nino held a silver coin tight in one hand. When the collection box, which was fastened on a long handle, came round to him, he put his coin in it, noticing at the same time that the box was almost full. He was glad when the kneeling was over, and he sat back in the seat and thought of God and Easter.

Easter mass was over. The peasants, all dressed in their best clothes, streamed out into the sunshine which flooded the square facing the church. They stood around, greeting and saluting one another. Color filled the square. The blue, red, yellow, and green dresses of the village women mixed with the sober gray and black of the men. The rich colors blended harmoniously with the somber gray walls of the church.

The priest, who had changed from his altar robes to a long black cassock with a row of buttons running all the way down the front, walked through the crowd and chatted with the village folks. Nino watched him talking with Signor Patri, the fat and jovial Mayor of the village. The priest was bareheaded; he fingered a long string of beads that hung almost to the ground and wore a silver cross that glittered in the morning sun.

"Good morning, Father Bellarosa," said Nino as the priest turned from Signor Patri and walked towards the little group made up of Signor Ditto, the Signora, Julio, Jacobo the artist, the butcher, the cobbler, and Nino's best friend the pastrycook. These and many more had been asked to come up to Casa Checchi for the feast.

"How are you, Nino?" said the priest. "How are you this fine Easter Day?" And he patted Nino's curly head.

"Oh, I'm so excited!" said Nino. "I'm so glad that you are coming to dinner today. I want to show you the rooster you gave me. It's still as good as new."

"All right, Nino. I'll be there. I would not miss your mother's cooking for anything, especially her baking," he said to Nino, as he walked over to talk with another group of villagers.

Nino was very fond of kind Father Bellarosa. He seldom scolded him at catechism and, besides, hadn't he given him the best toy he had?

Pigeons flew in and out of the belfry. Nino watched them circle the campanile and disappear in the rafters of the tower. Nino had been up in the tower once. He remembered how dizzy it made him feel when he looked down. He wondered if the pigeons didn't sometimes feel dizzy, too. Nino didn't like the way they stood around on the peaks of the roof and the eaves. Just then a pigeon alighted safely on the cross on top of the tower, and Nino knew why God had made wings.

Julio came up to where Nino stood, still looking upwards.

[116]

"What are you looking at?" asked Julio. "Haven't you ever seen the campanile before?"

"Yes, I have," said Nino. "I was just noticing how well the pigeons take care of themselves. See that one perched up on the cross?" he said pointing. "He's not at all frightened."

"They have wings, haven't they? I don't see why you worry about such things," said Julio, shrugging his shoulders.

A shy girl about Nino's age stood beside Julio. She was dressed in red, and a white embroidered apron fitted tightly high above her waist.

"Nino, this is my cousin, Gloria. She came all the way from Florence to spend a month with us," said Julio. "Won't we have fun now!" he said, jumping up and down like a marionette.

"I like the apron you're wearing, Gloria," said Nino. "Did your mother make it?"

"No, Nino," said Gloria in a shy voice. "It was bought for me in Florence."

Nino knew that Florence was a large city. He hoped that some day his mother would take him there. He had heard of all the fine things one could see in that "City of the Arts," which was what Grandfather often called Florence.

"Grandfather," said Nino, "may I go to Julio's house with him? He wants to stop for his new mandolin."

"Wait," said Signor Ditto. "There's something I want too."

"All right, Nino. Don't be long, though. Your mother is

probably waiting for us all to come now," said the old man.

The four hurried off to the Dittos'. Julio found his mandolin, and his father went into the cellar and came out with an armful of bottles.

"*Viva il vino!* Hurray for wine!" he shouted, the bottles clinking against one another.

The four were panting with haste when they entered the courtyard. The long table stood under the wide grape arbor, covered with a coarse linen tablecloth which Nino's mother had woven on her loom.

There was already a large gathering of villagers in the courtyard. They talked and gesticulated, moving their arms, shrugging their shoulders, and occasionally glancing in the direction of the oven and the table. Allinda was bringing out huge bowls of thick soup and Signora Ditto followed with platters of bread cut in thick slices.

Julio went around poking his nose into this and that while Nino and Gloria walked over to the oven. The door was shut.

"Can't guess what's in there," Nino said to Gloria.

"Let's peek," she said.

Nino, with a finger to his mouth, said: "Sh!"

He opened the door of the oven just a little and they both peeked in.

"Um, um, that smells good!" said Gloria.

Nino's mother arrived just in time to give Nino a gentle box on the ear.

"Poky nose," she said.

[118]

"Mother, this is Gloria. She is Julio's cousin from Florence."

Allinda made a bow to the little girl and said: "We are happy to have you with us."

"I wonder why the pastrycook is so late," said Nino. "And the cobbler, he is late too," he added.

Julio said: "I'm hungry."

"Oh, they'll be here any minute," said Allinda as she walked toward the priest, who was shaking hands with the fat Signora Ditto for the second time that day.

"I didn't see you at mass today," said the good priest, pointing an accusing finger at Allinda. "Too busy with all this?" he said, waving a hand about the courtyard.

"No, Father," said Allinda. "I was at the early mass."

The old priest gave Allinda a gentle pat on the cheek and said: "My eyes are getting bad. I'm getting old, I guess."

Finally both the pastrycook and the cobbler arrived and everyone sat down to eat. Grandfather sat at one end of the huge table and the priest at the other. The jovial Mayor was placed in the middle with his dark-eyed wife by his side. Corrina and Pietro, their children, sat one on each side of them. Signor and Signora Ditto were across the table from the Mayor. Julio sat between Gloria and Nino, next to Grandfather. Friends of Grandfather and Allinda filled the rest of the table.

Father Bellarosa stood up. The kind priest raised one hand heavenward and while those seated about the long table bowed their heads he said: "O Lord in heaven, bless this food, and give strength to those who partake of it. Amen." Little shafts of sunlight streamed through the leaves from the arbor above.

Immediately after the priest had finished saying grace, Julio announced in a loud voice: "The soup smells good!"

Gloria giggled, and Nino said: "Hush!"

The priest sat down, smiling, and helped himself to the soup. The two huge bowls were soon emptied.

Signor Ditto said: "Don't put all the grated cheese in your soup, Julio."

Julio handed the cheese to Gloria, who in turn handed it to Nino.

"I like my soup plain," she said.

"A little cheese makes the soup taste better," Nino replied.

Grandfather rose and, holding his glass, said: "*Salute!* A happy Easter to all, and *salute* to Signor Ditto," he added, "who brought us this good old vintage."

Everyone except the children drank the wine.

Nino said to Gloria: "When I grow up, I'll drink wine too."

Julio told Gloria that he knew what wine tasted like.

Ravioli were served next. The little shells of dough filled with minced vegetables and chicken meat, and covered with brown mushroom sauce, were heaped high on huge terracotta platters.

"Oh!" said Julio. "That smells even better than the soup!"

Grandfather gave Julio a good plateful of ravioli, which disappeared fast. Everyone ate and enjoyed each other's company. The food was good, and all the guests praised Allinda's cooking.

Julio said: "Mother, why don't you make ravioli like these?"

Signora Ditto blushed a deep red and Signor Ditto looked daggers at his son.

The rack of lamb came out of the oven steaming hot and roasted to a juicy brown. Allinda cut the rack into chops. Heaps of fried squash, fried quail, and chicken followed.

"Isn't it a grand meal!" said Nino to Gloria, as he picked out a nice fat drum stick and put it on Gloria's plate.

Gloria smiled and said: "Thank you, Nino. I like the drum stick best of all the chicken."

Nino was pleased.

"Pass me a gizzard," Julio said to Nino, and Nino looked about the platter for a gizzard, found one, stuck it with his fork, and put it on Julio's plate. "Don't you like gizzards?" Julio asked Gloria. "It's the chicken's stomach, you know. My mother found a penny in one once. The chicken had swallowed it."

In spite of his many threats, Grandfather after all had not had the heart to sacrifice his pet rooster for the Easter

feast. The bird, with his flock of hens beside him, strutted about the courtyard now, occasionally sidling near the table to pick up a stray fallen crumb. Once in a while he crowed triumphantly, as though he had known all along that Grandfather would never put him in the oven, and the old man, picking on a chicken wing, thought how good it was to hear his voice still.

Caesar prowled round impatiently. He had to wait until the table was cleared before he would get his share.

The bones were removed from the plates before each person, and a big bowl of curly lettuce with chopped onions and garlic was passed around. Each guest stirred the oil and red vinegar at the bottom of the bowl before helping himself.

But the children had eaten so much already that they shook their heads at the salad.

Julio leaned toward Gloria and said: "Now comes the part *I* like best!"

The table was covered with cakes and tarts and sliced panettone. The men dipped the slices in wine and ate them that way. The children fell upon the roosters and soldiers first, then went after the smaller cookies.

Julio, saying: "I begin to feel not so good," took a large piece of the squash tart.

Signora Ditto said: "Julio, you'll be sick. Don't make such a glutton of yourself."

Julio replied: "Oh, Ma!" his mouth so full it was all but running over.

Gloria, too, thought that Julio was overeating.

"Don't you think so?" she asked Nino.

"I don't know," said Nino. "Julio can eat an awful lot without feeling it. I remember the time when we ate green grapes together. I was sick, but he didn't even get a tummy ache."

Black coffee came next, along with cheese, nuts, and candy which the pastrycook had brought from his shop. The food was beginning to tell on some of the guests. They stretched their legs, belched politely, and loosened their sashes. The meal had lasted two hours. The children were the first to leave the table. Their elders still lingered over their coffee cups. The bottle of cognac went up and down the table. Almost everyone took a little in the black coffee.

Signor Ditto drank a toast to the house of Checchi, and Nino felt very proud indeed.

The afternoon sun hung bright over Casa Checchi and the shadow cast by the house crept slowly over the courtyard towards the arbor.

Nino and Gloria stood on the stone terrace overlooking the village and the lowland below.

"Massarosa is a beautiful village," said Gloria. "What is that shining in the distance?" she asked Nino, pointing to the west.

"Don't you know?" said Nino. "That's the Mediterranean and right near it is Viareggio. There's Pietrasanta over there to the right and there," said Nino, pointing to the east, "is Ponte Vecchio; and there's 'le Cappane.' Look right at the end of that long canal. See the two tall poplars, one on each side?"

Gloria said: "My, what a lot of things you can see from here!"

The towns in the lowlands were dotted here and there. They looked like minute toy villages in the distance.

"You see those big gashes in the hillside?" said Nino. "Those are the Carrara marble quarries. Michelangelo and Donatello once quarried their marble there. They were the two greatest sculptors of the Renaissance. My mother told me so. I'm going to be an artist like Jacobo when I grow up," he told Gloria confidently.

Unheeded, the two gazed over the landscape. Gloria shaded her eyes from the slanting rays of the sun. Nino

thought she looked beautiful standing there with the sun
lighting her hair to a rich golden color.

Terraces stretched out below them, terraces that had been
built by the peasants piling stone on stone to wall up the
land. Onions, garlic, peppers, turnips, lettuce, and little
patches of herbs were grown there.

Allinda's garden lay just below them. It went around the

back of the tall stone house. Olive trees hooded the hillside between the village and the house. They could see Signor Ditto's vineyard from here too, and his house that stood at the edge of it. The little village lay below them bathed in sunshine. Its narrow streets and square stone stuccoed houses and shops were mellowed with age, gray and somber in tone. Only the red tile roofs looked new.

The tuning of instruments brought the two to attention. Music filled the air. Gloria and Nino turned to see the courtyard in shadow. The villagers were singing. Some still sat at the table. Julio was nowhere to be seen.

"Where's Julio?" Nino asked his mother, looking towards the children who had gathered in a group playing a game.

"Julio is in bed," said Allinda. "He ate too much and became so ill that we had to give him some medicine. He'll be all right in a little while."

Nino scratched his head; Gloria began to giggle, and put her hand over her mouth.

"It's no wonder," she said. "He ate an awful lot for anyone his size."

The musicians were all neighboring friends. Jacobo played the violin, Signor Ditto the piccolo, the cobbler a clarinet, and the pastrycook the accordion. They all played well. Nino had heard them before. Signor Ditto's piccolo with its high-pitched notes could be heard much above the other instruments. They were playing a mazurka, gay and fast. The Mayor had coaxed his dark-eyed young wife to dance, and others followed. The dancers whirled and spun in circles, bouncing up and down and keeping time with the music. Clapping of hands, singing voices, and shouts filled the air, and the courtyard echoed with merriment. The children joined hands in a large circle. Around and around they went, with Nino holding tightly to Gloria. Even Grandfather's rooster joined in the excitement, flapping his wings and crowing loudly.

Julio could be seen up at the window, his face the picture of misery.

Calling to his mother, he said in a loud voice: "The medicine's working!"

His mother shouted back: "Serves you right for making a pig of yourself!" and went on dancing with one of the younger men.

The musicians played many pieces, among them a tarantella in which the peasants dance singly at first, holding one hand on the hip and tapping first one foot and then the other.

Nino saw Signor Ditto drop his piccolo and take Allinda by the hand. They joined the dancing couples. Nino knew his mother was a good dancer, lighter on her feet than any of the others.

With the setting of the sun, the music subsided and the tolling of the church bells told Nino that Father Bellarosa had left the party to perform the evening vesper service. The villagers knelt in the courtyard and with bowed heads said a long prayer, while the soft mellow tones of the bells rang out in the dusk.

A large fire built of fagots was started in the courtyard, and the group sat around it and talked. The children huddled against their parents. Nino, who was sitting next to Gloria, gazed into the flames.

"What do you see in the flames, Nino?" said Gloria.

"Oh, there are lots of things to be seen in the flames if you use your imagination," said Nino. "Right now I see two red giants fighting, and then over on that side, where the smaller flames are, I see a flock of roosters pecking at one another. See, see?" he said pointing.

Gloria peered into the fire.

"I don't see any roosters, Nino. I see people dancing and they are all dressed in gorgeous red robes," she said excitedly.

"You see the devil dancing in there," said Signor Ditto, who had been listening to the conversation.

"Oh, Signor Ditto! I can't see what you see at all," said Nino laughing.

"Oh, yes, you can if you look hard enough. Look, look. There he is now, right at the top. That big flame. There, see? Isn't that the demon? See his tail whipping about the air?" said Signor Ditto again.

"Don't believe a word he says to you," said Signora Ditto. "He's always poking fun."

The Signor laughed, gave a whistle, and hugged his fat wife.

"Ditto, Ditto," said the fat Signora, "stop being a boy and grow up."

The children laughed and clapped their hands at the two. Strains of a tinkling mandolin came from the direction of the house.

Allinda said: "Julio must be feeling better."

Julio joined the group around the fire. The villagers teased him, till he hung his head in shame. But he soon recovered his usual spirits, and played them a piece on his mandolin by way of atonement.

The pale moon looked down on the group around the fire from a crest of the dark hills above. The children roasted chestnuts in the hot coals. Now and then there was a loud pop. One had exploded. The children went: "Boom, boom, boom!" after each report. Tales were told by the villagers as they sat smoking their pipes. As the fire burned low, the children huddled closer to their parents. A candlelight threw a faint beam from a window in Casa Checchi. The voices of the people around the fire became almost like whispers. The stars hung in the heavens like flickering candles. Jacobo played his violin. Deep sad tones stole away into the night, making tears come into Nino's eyes. He wiped them away with the back of his hand.

As Nino and his mother went indoors, Allinda said: "Why, Nino, you've been crying! What's wrong? Tell me."

"Oh, Mother," said Nino with tears streaming down his cheeks, "I—I love Jacobo's violin music so much that it makes me cry!"

"There, there, you old silly," said his mother affectionately.

But she understood. The festivities, meeting Gloria—the whole day had been too much for him.

As Nino lay in his bed that night, he heard Signor Ditto's voice ringing in the night. It came from somewhere below Casa Checchi. It echoed in the glens of the hillside; fainter and fainter it sounded and finally was lost in the night. Silence filled the room.

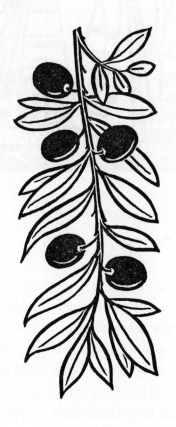

CHAPTER VIII

HARVEST

WITH August came the ripening of the olives. The grapes had been gathered and the corn would be harvested after the olives were picked. The hillside below Casa Checchi was shrouded in a silvery gray. The men up in the olive trees sang as they picked, and their voices filled the morning air. They sang to the young women below them. With linen bags about their waists, the women and children raked through the grass, filling their bags. Huge baskets filled with the dark, shining olives stood under the trees.

Nino, on his knees beside his mother, searched through the grass, picking up the olives and putting them into his mother's linen bag.

Nino said to his mother: "Look! The 'Three Brothers.' I thought they would come soon."

Three monks with shaven heads bent as if in benediction were making their way through the grove. They had come from the monastery up on the hill. They went over to Grandfather, who was sitting on an overturned wicker basket under the trees.

"God bless your crop," they said, making the sign of the cross over the baskets already filled with olives.

Nino saw one of the monks, the fattest one, take a handful of the fruit and let it fall from his hand back into the basket.

"A good crop, indeed," said the fat monk to Grandfather.

"We are thankful," Grandfather replied.

The Three Brothers, as the village people called them, were always to be seen together, going about with sacks on their shoulders. They went from house to house, receiving a little of this and a little of that. On their return to the monastery, they were often loaded down like pack mules.

Now they stood holding open their sacks. Grandfather filled each half full of olives. The three blessed the old man at once and made their way out of the grove.

Nino said: "Grandfather is generous today."

[133]

"He is always generous, Nino," his mother replied.

Nino watched the monks shuffling their sandaled feet through the grass. Their hoods hung like knapsacks down their backs as they disappeared down the hill toward the village.

Nino looked up to see the setting sun throwing fantastic lights and shadows among the leaves of the huge trees. Through an opening, Nino saw the golden disk sinking far toward the western horizon. The gray leaves of the olive trees turned slowly into glittering silver. The breeze played gently with the quivering leaves. They sparkled like crystals in the waning sunlight.

The young men took the baskets into Grandfather's storehouse. Tomorrow they would be sorted. The little, green olives would be taken out and put into kegs of salt brine and cinnamon to sweeten them.

That night Allinda made a stew of lamb and ripe olives. It tasted good to Nino with the hot polenta.

"Why do the monks beg?" Nino asked his grandfather during the evening meal.

"They are so busy praying and making the rounds of blessings, they probably haven't time to do anything else. It's a custom of the monks to receive charity in return for their blessings."

"They make their own wine, though," said Nino. "Don't they?"

Many times he had seen the heavily laden arbors that shade the courtyard of the monastery.

"They make sacramental wine. You know, the kind
Father Bellarosa drinks during mass."

"And during meals too," said Allinda.

"It's good wine the monks make." And with a wink that
was meant for Allinda, Grandfather added: "The Three
Brothers will come to bless our corn next week. You'll see
them sorting out the largest ears."

Next morning mellow, deep-toned echoes from the
church bells vibrated in the morning air. Grandfather's pet
rooster, who had been strutting about the courtyard since
the first light of dawn, crowed loudly.

"It's time to get up," said Nino, stretching his arms until
he thought they would snap. "Oh, I'm stiff. It's from the
picking yesterday, I guess," he said, putting on his shoes.

[135]

He leaned out of the window and shouted: "Hello, Grandfather! I can't see you."

From beneath a huge bundle of fagots, Grandfather shouted back: "Hello! It's time you were up. Better hurry if you want to help with the sorting."

But before Nino could answer, Grandfather had taken the huge bundle into the house.

"Hurry, Nino. Breakfast is ready. Hurry. It's going to be a busy day."

The storehouse was filled with neighbors who had come to help with the day's work.

"Look at that boy sort olives," said Allinda to Grand-father. "He is getting to be a real help to us."

Nino's nimble fingers went through the olives like light-ning, selecting the little, green ones from the black, ripe ones. He put the green olives into a small keg.

The sorters sat at long tables chatting, occasionally chid-ing one another jovially. Nino saw some of the young men making eyes at the young women. Sometimes the young women would tease the young men. This flustered them so that they would put the green olives where the ripe ones should be.

The sorting lasted all day long, and by sundown Nino's hands were stained a strange brown color. His fingers had the smell of rancid oil on them. It would be three or four days before the stain and smell would disappear.

The following day the miller came with his donkey cart and took the ripe olives to the mill to be crushed into olive oil.

"Come, Nino," said Grandfather. "Let's walk down to the mill. I want to see that the olives get a good crushing."

Nino had heard that the miller was not to be trusted. He often left oil in the mash for himself.

They went to the mill by way of a path that led through the olive grove. Nino saw the poorer peasants of the village raking through the grass in search of stray olives that had been left behind. Nino hoped they would fine plenty.

"Be careful of the branches," said Grandfather to a young boy high up on a slender limb who was trying to get some

[137]

olives far beyond his reach. "Be careful of the branches. Don't snap them," said Grandfather.

They passed old grandmas and grandpas on their knees in the grass. Nino felt sorry for them. He wished they too had olive trees and corn fields like his grandfather's.

"The olive trees are beautiful today, Grandfather," Nino said, full of enthusiasm. "God did a grand thing when He made the olive tree, didn't He?"

"Yes, He did," said the old man. "The olive branch has been the emblem of peace for generations, and the olive oil—think of that—your mother could not make risotto which you are so fond of without olive oil."

"And she couldn't make risotto without rice, either," said Nino, laughing.

They entered the old mill, which stood at the edge of a chestnut grove a little above the Church of Santa Lucia. Its walls, once white, had weathered to an ashen gray during its long years of service to the olive growers of the countryside. A rancid odor filled the atmosphere. The old mill had been soaked in oil for years.

Nino listened to the muffled footsteps of the oxen on the upper floor. They went round and round, turning the huge stone crusher over the olives. He could hear the miller's helper, a hunch-backed old man, goading the oxen round and round on the floor above. The olives made a "grash, grash" noise as the heavy stone roller went over them. Nino, his eyes bright with excitement, was all over the mill at once: first upstairs to help with the oxen, then downstairs to follow

the stone roller on its never-varying routine round and round.

Grandfather leaned over the stone mortar and took up a handful of mashed olives. This he examined very carefully, using in turn the sense of smell, sight, and touch.

"The mash looks fine to me," he said to the miller. "We can go ahead with the pressing now."

With much sputtering the miller called for his man upstairs to stop the oxen and come down. The miller then rolled his greasy trousers up over his hairy shins and above his knees. He climbed into the mortar. With a wooden shovel he filled hempen containers that stood in shallow kegs, while the hunch-back who had clambered into the mortar after him held the sides open. They filled the containers with the oily mash until the mortar was clean. Then they put more ripe olives into the mortar and the hunch-back went upstairs again.

Nino watched eagerly every move of the miller's hands. The hempen containers, closely tied up, were lifted into a heavy wooden press. One over the other the containers were piled. When six stood in the press, a heavy wooden board was placed over the pile. A strong iron screw with a huge twist went round and round. The veins on the strong arms of the miller became bigger and bigger, as he strained against the turn screw. Nino thought they couldn't get much bigger or they would burst. The pressure from the screw crushed the hempen containers together tightly and the oil flowed slowly down the sides of the press and into a vat below. Nino, watching, wondered why the same method was not used in making wine. Grandfather said it couldn't be done without crushing the seed in the grapes.

"That makes bad wine when you crush the seed," he said to Nino. "You get bad wine. It makes it bitter."

The crushing and pressing came to an end.

"Your trees yielded well this year, Padrone. Last year you got exactly forty gallons. This year you get ten more gallons. Plenty of oil," said the miller.

"Plenty there is." Grandfather replied.

He measured the oil with a long stick with notches cut in it.

"I just want to make sure there's fifty gallons," he said to the miller.

On their way home they passed Julio's house. A donkey cart filled with grapes stood in the courtyard.

"Signor Ditto is making wine," said Nino. "Can we stop in for just a moment, Grandfather?"

"Let's do so. It is still early," agreed Grandfather.

Nino found Julio leaning over a barrel. Tiny flies swarmed over his head. They were wine flies.

"What are you doing, Julio?" said Nino.

"Oh, just sucking some grape juice through this straw. Try some, Nino."

He handed Nino a straw. Nino sucked up some of the juice and, making a wry face, spat it out again.

"Ugh!" he said. "It doesn't taste very good, does it?"

"I like it," said Julio, leaning over the barrel again to sip up more of the fresh grape juice.

[141]

"You may get drunk," warned Nino, "if you drink too much. Be careful."

"Oh, no. You can't get drunk. It has to ferment first."

In the big wine vat Signor Ditto, up to his knees in purple grapes, was stamping up and down, smashing the grapes into a mash. The juice foamed about his legs, and Nino could smell the sour-sweet smell of the grape skins that swirled and bubbled with each stamp of Signor Ditto's feet.

"There, that batch is done."

He climbed out of the barrel and went to the well, where he washed the red stains from his legs and feet.

Putting on his zoccoli, the wooden shoes he wore at work, he said: "Come into the cellar, Padrone. I have some of the old vintage left. You know, the kind I brought you when Nino was baptized."

"Thanks, Ditto. I can't refuse any of that. Don't think it will spoil my appetite, either, do you?"

"No, it will give more, much more appetite, Padrone," Signor Ditto assured him with a hearty clap on the back, as they went into the cellar.

Julio, who by now had his fill of grape juice, called to Nino: "The sow has had little ones. I'll show them to you."

The two boys walked off to the pig pen.

Grandfather and Signor Ditto sat in the cool cellar and discussed the problems peculiar to wine making.

Grandfather said: "If you know the right time to change the wine from one barrel to another, you will always have good wine. Also the stars have a great deal to do with it."

"You are right," said Signor Ditto. "I have tasted wine that was made by machine. It's not half as good as wine made with the feet. But," said Signor Ditto, rubbing his legs, which were beginning to itch from the grape juice, and pointing a finger at Grandfather, "but if they make the proper machine, it will make the proper wine."

Grandfather said: "Oh, fiddlesticks. Ditto! I say the old methods are the best. You can depend on them. Wine made by machine—it isn't possible."

"The right kind of machine will make good wine," insisted Signor Ditto.

"Fiddlesticks! Ditto, when that day comes, there will be no good wine left to drink."

He held up a glass of red wine as he spoke.

"*Salute, buona salute*," he said. "And here's to the day of the machines. May they never come to our village!"

He put his empty glass down.

"Signor Ditto," Grandfather went on in a solemn voice, "they say that in America everything is done with machinery. The whole country is filled with machinery of all kinds. They do everything with the infernal things."

Signor Ditto listened while scratching his legs, which still itched.

"My son-in-law told me in a letter from there that the machine was starting a new age in industry. He told me that he worked in a factory where they made nothing but tin cans. They put a flat piece of tin into a machine. Whir, whir, and a round tin can rolls out. Mind you, all finished too. They make millions and millions of tin cans a day. They have factories for everything in America."

"America must be a wonderful place," said Signor Ditto. "It must be a wonderful place from the stories you hear about that country. I wonder what the farmers in America will do when machinery comes."

Grandfather replied that he had heard they were making more and more horseless carriages every day. Soon there would be no use for the horse, except for pleasure riding.

"Too bad," said Signor Ditto. "I love to work with horses, don't you, Padrone? They're so understanding."

"Yes. If machinery comes," said the old man, "more and more machines will follow. More and newer inventions will be thought of. It will be the beginning of a new age in our civilization too. The infernal things will infest the entire face of the earth. We may even have them here in this village. Think of it!" said Grandfather getting more and more worked up. "Think of it! No more looking to nature for food. Maybe machinery will make food for us. I don't know what the machine will mean to us all here if it ever comes."

Grandfather's glass had been refilled during his outburst on the future. He held the glass high in the air once more.

"*Salute, Signor Ditto,*" he said. "Here's to our old age. 'Youth is short, old age long.'"

The two touched glasses and drank.

A sound of grunting and squealing came from the direction of the pig pen.

Signor Ditto stuck his head out of the cellar door and shouted: "Julio! Stop teasing the sow. You know she has little ones."

Nino and Julio came to the entrance of the cellar. A baby pig was squealing as he tried to free himself from Julio's clutches. The boy continued to hold him tightly in his arms.

"Father, may I give this one to Nino? He hasn't any baby pigs. He wants it. Please, may I give it to him?"

Signor Ditto nodded his head. "You may have him, Nino, if your grandfather doesn't mind feeding another one."

"I'll feed him myself," said Nino. "Thanks, Signor Ditto and Julio. When he grows too big, you can have him back."

[145]

Signor Ditto went back to his wine making and Julio helped bring grapes from the donkey cart. The peaceful donkey, grown impatient, had been sitting on his hind end in the courtyard for an hour waiting for someone to help him up.

"It was good of Julio to give me the baby pig," said Nino as they made their way up the path that led to Casa Checchi.

When Nino neared the house, he let the baby pig go. It made straight for the door and into the house, with squeaky high-pitched grunts. Once in the room, the little pig stood still and looked about him, his beady little eyes sparkling, his tail switching back and forth excitedly. Nino picked him up and he lay quietly in Nino's arms.

"Look, Mother," he said. "He is an unusual pig. See how tame he is. He is all white, too, except for this black ear. We'll always be able to tell him from the others."

"Nino, of all things to bring into the house!" Allinda exclaimed. "Put him right in the pen with the other pigs."

"Oh, Mother," said Nino. "But he is a special pig. I'm going to keep him for a pet. He'll behave and he seems to like it so here in the house. Please, Mother."

Allinda said: "We are not going to have any pigs, not even a special pig, walking about the house. They do it in Naples but it's not done in Massarosa."

"What can I do with him?" said Nino, disappointed.

"Come, son, we'll make a pen for him under the oven and perhaps you can tame him so that he will eat out of your hand," said Grandfather.

"He is not to stay in the house. Get out, all of you!" cried Allinda, fanning her apron at them.

Grandfather, Nino, and the pig went silently through the door. Grandfather put a wall of fagots around the pillars that supported the oven.

Nino said: "There, Piggy, you will have a nice home of your own. Good night."

That night Allinda was awakened by a series of shrill squeals, punctuated by occasional grunts. The commotion seemed to come from Nino's room. Leaving her bed and hurrying in there, she lighted a candle and found Nino with his eyes tightly shut and to all appearances sound asleep. His arms were tightly clasped around the tiny pig, who was struggling mightily to free himself.

"Nino, Nino!" said Allinda. "Wake up! Wake up!"

Nino opened his eyes slowly, as though he had been asleep.

[147]

"Oh, Mother," he said. "Piggy fell out of bed, and while I was looking for him in the dark I stepped on his tail. That's probably what woke you up."

Grandfather lay in his bed, shaking with laughter. He knew that Nino had taken the pig to bed with him.

"I thought Grandfather made a pen for him under the oven," said Allinda. "How did he get from the pen into your bed? That's what I want to know!"

Nino offered no explanation. Allinda didn't want the pig in the house, and told Nino that she meant it. Nino, now very crestfallen, put on his trousers and took the pig out to the pen under the oven. His mother saw that the pig was safely bedded down on a heap of straw in a corner of the enclosure.

"Now you go right up to bed and remember, no pigs in the house," said his mother, "or back to the Dittos' he goes. Mind you don't bring him in the house again."

Nino said: "All right, Mother." And he went back to bed.

He lay awake thinking about the little pig. He must be cold, thought Nino, and slipping from his bed he went and stood by the window. Everything in the courtyard was clearly outlined by the moonlight. Nino could hear the baby pig stirring about in the pen Grandfather had made for him. Aside from this slight rustling there was nothing to be heard, either indoors or out. The sound of his elbows scraping against the windowsill as he leaned there startled Nino for an instant. He was more cautious in moving about after that. He looked up at the moon, and then at the oven. Mak-

[148]

ing his mind up suddenly, Nino put on his trousers and blouse and went quietly down the stairs. The moon outside followed him to the oven.

"Why do you follow me?" Nino asked the moon.

His shadow also followed Nino to the oven.

He looked about the courtyard. It seemed as if he were walking in a dream. Everything was black and gray. Only the moon seemed cheerful. Nino reached into the pen for the baby pig.

"Where are you?" he said, stretching his arms about the enclosure. "Come, Piggy, come."

The pig stirred in a corner. Making an opening in the fagots, Nino crawled in, and found the little pig lying in the straw almost out of sight. He sat by the pig, petting him now and then. The moon looked down to see a little pig clutched tightly in the arms of a little boy. And the moon smiled in the clear night.

"Come, Nino," called Allinda next morning. "Come. Wake up! Why don't you answer me?"

She turned the slices of polenta over on the grate.

"What's the matter with that boy? Too much pig last night," she said to herself as she went up to his room.

"Nino!" she cried on seeing the empty bed. "Where are you, Nino? Come! Your breakfast is ready."

Allinda looked about the room and, finding it empty, went to the window. The courtyard below showed no signs of life. Only the bright morning sun shone on the smooth earth. Startled, Allinda flew down the stairs.

"Father, Father!" she cried. "Nino has gone. Have you seen him?"

She shook Grandfather, who lay peacefully in his huge oaken bed. Allinda shook and shook him. Finally the old man sat up in his bed and, rubbing his eyes, said: "It certainly was a tremendous crop! Fifty gallons. I'll sell some of it at the Fair.

"Oh, good morning, daughter. What's the matter? Why are you waking me up so early? The rooster hasn't crowed yet, has he?"

Allinda stood by the bed.

Frantically she said: "Father, Nino is not in his bed!"

"What?" said the old man, springing out of the bed. "What? Not in his bed!"

"No," said Allinda. "He's gone. I know. I shouldn't have scolded him about the baby pig."

And she burst into tears.

"Now, now, Allinda," said the old man. "It's not as bad as you think. Perhaps he got up early and took the pig back to the Dittos'. Let's go and see if the pig is still in the pen."

Grandfather, with his shoes still unlaced and buttoning his shirt on the way to the pig pen, said: "Nino is much too sensible to run away from home because of a little scolding."

Allinda followed her father across the courtyard to the oven, wiping her eyes with her apron as she went. Peering through the fagots, Grandfather and Allinda saw Nino and the little pig asleep together under a heap of straw. Grandfather roared at the sight.

[150]

Allinda said: "I hope he hasn't caught a cold sleeping with the pig."

Grandfather continued to laugh and at last Allinda burst into laughter too. It woke Nino, who looked about him and brushed the straw that clung to his curly hair.

"Mother," he said. "Mother, I fell asleep!"

His mother, still laughing, said: "Come, Nino, your breakfast is waiting."

The baby pig, who was now awake too, squealed when Nino left him.

The night's adventure was over, but Nino had not yet heard the end of it. The following week at the corn husking, Signor Ditto said to him: "I hear you liked my pig so much that you went to sleep with him. Is that so?"

Nino evaded the question by saying: "The little pig eats right out of my hand now. You should see him, Signor Ditto. You should see the way he follows me everywhere excepting in the house," said Nino seriously. "Mother said the house is no place for pigs."

"That's right," said Signor Ditto. "The house is no place for pigs. Keep him out in the sunshine, feed him well, and when the Fair comes, perhaps you'll want to trade him for something you may like better."

The corn husking took place at "le Cappane." Men carried the corn in baskets from the fields, and threw it in large piles on the floor. Tearing sounds filled the huge room as the men and women tore the dry husks from the corn, leaving only two strands of husk to each ear. Long ropes hung from the eaves on the south wall of the building. Outside, Nino threw corn up to Signor Ditto, perched on a ladder, who tied one ear of corn over another, twisting the two husks around the rope. Soon the long festoons of corn ears shone like gold in the sun. Signor Ditto climbed higher and higher on the ladder, until one of the younger men had to come and throw the corn for Nino. After that, Nino went to the field with Julio in the donkey cart to gather more corn.

Julio shook his fist at the crows that flew over the cart always caw-cawing.

"They always fly low during harvest," he said. "And they're always hungry."

"If they haven't already eaten their fill," Nino answered, "they had better hurry. There won't be any left soon."

The donkey stood eating dry leaves from the tall stalks while the boys filled the cart with corn.

As they drove back they talked of the coming Fair.

"I wonder who'll win the wrestling contest with the gypsies' bear this year," said Nino.

"I don't know. Last year he threw everyone. My father said he thinks he knows the trick. My father is strong, Nino. He might win," said Julio.

Harvest was over and the corn was left on the long ropes to dry. Nino and Julio took turns each day at keeping the crows away from it. They had long sticks with flat pieces of wood tied at the end. Whenever a crow came near, they swung the stick around and around in a circle over their heads. It made a whir-whirring noise like that one makes by blowing across the opening of a bottle.

Grandfather paid off the neighbors who had helped him, either with corn, olive oil, wheat, or money. Most of them took their wages in kind, with perhaps a few pennies besides. Grandfather was generous with the help. He told them no one could live by bread alone and, besides, the Fair was coming. It had been a good year, and the peasants in the village were thankful to the land.

CHAPTER IX

THE FAIR

FROM the hillside Nino looked down on the village square below, a riot of color in the morning sun. The wind brought the sound of music played by the village brass band.

"Don't hurry so, Nino," said his grandfather. "You'll have the whole day to see everything at the Fair."

Allinda followed close behind her father and the eagerly hurrying child. She was dressed in her best crimson skirt and wore an embroidered blouse, emerald green in color, which was laced in crisscross fashion at the front. Her long

chestnut hair was tightly tied in a knot, over which she wore a bright yellow shawl.

Nino was all excitement as he walked along.

They entered the square, now the scene of much good-natured confusion with the music and the shouting and laughter of the people. The members of the village band, dressed in uniforms of scarlet, green, and gold, were seated under a canopy of red, white, and green bunting. Many flags of those same colors fluttered in the breeze. The band had stopped to rest, and the man who played the bass horn was wiping his brow. The people jostled one another to get first places at the various booths, where they thought fortune might smile on them.

Nino looked up and down the long rows of booths, wondering at what particular one the Dittos might be. Wheels of chance clicked around noisily. Jugglers wearing red tights and black blouses stood on a platform tossing as many as twelve balls in a circle in the air. They showed little apparent interest in the spectators gathered to watch them. Candy canes of bright colors, and walnuts and hazelnuts strung like beads, were hung in one booth. Another booth was filled with pottery of all sorts—bowls, jugs, pitchers, platters, and vases of every conceivable shape and combination of colors filled its shelves.

The man was shouting: "This way! This way! Now is the time to buy your wife a present. This way! This way! Buy her a set of new dishes!"

A fat man whose face reminded one of a rose in bloom sat at a table spinning glass. Fascinated, Nino stood and watched the man's hands, which looked as large as hams, working carefully and swiftly as he wove delicate and intricate patterns of colored glass around a large bottle. The man warmed his hands over a little oil flame. Around and up, then crosswise went the threads of colored glass, interlacing, weaving, and forming the complex design around the green bottle. Nino thought it must be wonderful to be able to do that, though he found it difficult to understand how a man with such large hands and thick fingers could make patterns of such daintiness.

Noticing Nino's interest, the glass spinner stopped working and, smiling at the boy, he said: "Here, take this," and

[156]

handed toward him a thin strand of glass, like a ribbon.

Nino drew back slightly and asked: "Won't it burn?"

"Oh, no," said the fat man. "Take it."

Nino reached out for the glass and found it was barely warm. He twisted it into a little bracelet. The man then took it and dipped it into a bowl of water.

"There," he said. "It's for you. You made it."

"Thank you," said the surprised Nino.

"Wait!" said the man. "Let me finish it for you."

Using little flat pieces of green and yellow glass, he worked them over the bracelet.

"It is perfect," said Nino. "Buttercups with green leaves all around them. Oh, thank you, Signor!"

Grandfather bought Allinda a tiny colored bottle to keep oil of cloves in. On special occasions, Allinda always rubbed a little oil of cloves behind her ears.

The band was playing the "Triumphal March" from Aïda. The capitano was importantly swinging an oversized baton which he held between his first finger and thumb. He waved it through the air with all his might. Nino thought it would fly from his hand any minute and hit the bass horn. The leader, with arms flying through the air and his long black mustache blowing about, bounced up and down, as the platform rocked and swayed, keeping time with the music. The capitano's feathered hat, which didn't begin to fit him properly, persisted in settling on his shoulder rather than on his head.

"It's wonderful music, Mother," said Nino, "but I'm

[157]

afraid the capitano is going to be dead tired by nighttime."

"The capitano never gets tired, Nino. He's been training his band for three days without stopping in preparation for today. The capitano is an energetic man."

They moved about in the crowd looking for the Dittos.

"They must be here," said Nino. "Julio told me only yesterday that his father had given him a goat to trade for anything he wished for at the Fair."

The Fair was the scene of a great deal of trading every year. If someone began by trading a pig for a goat, by night he might find himself with either a new pipe or a milkless cow.

They found Julio at last, standing before a booth filled with alarm clocks. Large and small ones, highly plated and shining brightly in the sun, were ranged in rows on shelves covered in red bunting.

The proprietor was shouting: "Come, my dear folks! Here is something brand new. It rings the hour. Step up and inspect them for yourself. They're fresh from America. Something new and unusual. You'll need one sooner or later. Buy it now. Two lire, only two. Take one home with you."

Julio said: "I'll trade you my goat for one, Signor."

The man looked the goat over carefully, opened its mouth wide, felt its stomach, and said: "It's a bargain."

"Julio! Don't you do it. Your father will be angry," said Nino. "The goat is worth many times more than the clock. It gives milk, while the clock only tells time. Come away. You can make a better trade at some other booth."

The man with the alarm clocks was about to give Nino a box on the ear, and might have done so if it hadn't been for Grandfather, who stepped between the two.

"Come, boys," he said. "Let's see if the gypsies have arrived. They are late this year. And be careful of the sharpers," he added to the boys.

"Oh, I hope the gypsies come," said Nino. "It's so much fun. I hope the bear hasn't grown any bigger."

"They will be here any minute," said a man from Massa Carrara. "I saw their wagons along the road."

"Did you see the bear too?" asked Julio and Nino together.

"No, I didn't," said the man. "I didn't see any bears. Just gypsies."

He winked slyly at Grandfather and passed on through the crowd. A baby watching two acrobats turning cart wheels was crying at the top of his voice. Julio, with the goat tied by a rope to his waist, walked from booth to booth with Nino. At every booth there was something or other Julio wanted.

"No, no, Julio. Not that," Nino kept saying. "It's not worth half a goat!"

Grandfather and Allinda had found the Dittos, who stood chatting with the Mayor and the priest. The Mayor's wife had on earrings that looked as big as bracelets. They dangled from her ears and lighted up her dark skin. The Mayor, fat and jovial, stood by her side holding a gold-headed cane swordwise on his shoulder.

"Now, when I was in the cavalry," he was saying, "the

band played on horseback. And," he added, pointing to the municipal band with his cane, "they played much, much better than that."

The band had stopped to rest again. The voices of the people sounded louder than ever. Every shout, yell, and burst of laughter echoed against the façade of the church. The merry-go-round had just been set up. The owners of the contraption, having forgotten some of the parts, had had to go back three villages to find what they had left behind. The merry-go-round had been running just an hour now. A carabiniere dressed in a bright uniform was watching the merry-go-round. Julio and Nino stood beside the officer.

He knew the boys and said: "Hello, how would you two like a ride on the merry-go-round?"

"I have no money," said Julio, and looking down at his goat he asked the officer in all seriousness: "How many rides do you think I could get in exchange for him?"

"I don't know, but your goat would be a fair exchange for the entire outfit," said the officer. "I'll buy you each a ride," he said, smiling. "Wait till it stops before you get on," he cautioned the two excited boys.

Up went Nino and Julio. They sat on dilapidated steeds that had once been bright with color and trappings. The wooden horses, fastened to the roof by long iron rods, swayed and tottered from side to side. A new organ stood in the center of the merry-go-round. It played over and over again the popular songs of the day. Two donkeys were hitched to the merry-go-round to pull it around. Nino and Julio sat capering on the backs of the wooden steeds. The officer, still holding on to Julio's goat, and feeling a little dizzy from watching the motion of the merry-go-round, waved and called to the boys each time they passed. The owner of the merry-go-round finally called out in a very loud voice to the trotting donkeys. They slowed down and then halted. The ride was over. Nino and Julio leaped down and, after thanking the officer both for the ride and for holding the goat, they hurried off in the crowd.

There were shouts of "Here come the gypsies! Here come the gypsies!" The villagers made way for the band of gypsies, with their dark skins, flashing white teeth, and grinning

faces. The group, dressed in gay colors, made its way slowly through the crowd, headed by a tall handsome man with a bright red bandanna tied tightly over his head. He was dressed in velvet trousers of a deep brown shade, and wore tiny gold earrings and a purple sash round his waist. A huge shaggy bear, with a strong leather muzzle over his mouth and nose and a heavy studded collar around his neck, was walking on his hind legs behind the man. The big animal looked from side to side but seemed to ignore the staring crowd entirely. All the children and many of the older people rushed to that corner of the fair grounds which had been reserved for the gypsies. Here one might have his fortune told, his pots and pans mended, and, if he was not careful, perhaps his pocket picked as well. Here also was where the wrestling match was to take place between the bear and any man who might be brave enough to tackle him.

Nino said: "My, but the bear has grown much bigger! He is ever so much larger than he was last year. No one will be able to throw him. I hope no one tries to wrestle him."

"My father," said Julio, unwinding the goat's rope that had become tangled round his legs, "my father said that he would throw the bear this year, even if it gave him aches for ten years to come."

"I hope he will be careful," said Nino. "If your father gets mad, the bear will—and then maybe the gypsy will have to call the bear off."

"I don't know," said Julio. "My father is a strong man. He can lift a twenty-gallon cask of wine right onto his shoulders without even breathing heavily afterwards."

"But the bear is heavier than that, Julio. You see the size of him, and look at the big paws he has. I'd hate to get hit with one of them."

"Oh, well. We will see. My father said that if the bear came to the Fair, he would wrestle with him."

The gypsies settled themselves at the appointed place set aside for them by the Mayor. They squatted around the man with the bear. The animal sat licking his paws through the muzzle. He peered about the crowd, swaying his head first this way, then that, as if looking for some particular person in the group of people. Many of the villagers went home to fetch their pots and pans which required mending or polishing. Others just stood about and stared at the gypsies.

It was nearing the noon hour and the crowd had thinned out to some extent. Less noise came from the square and the owners of the booths shouted less heartily. Most of the village folk had gone home for their midday meal. The municipal band, however, played on during the lull in the Fair. The less noise in the square, the louder and faster the band played. The capitano was now perspiring freely as the result of his spirited leadership.

A huge tent had been pitched on the shaded side of the church, and was quickly filled by the village people and visitors. Long tables had been set up, at which one could buy food and drink.

Nino, his mother, and his grandfather sat with the Dittos near the end of one of the long tables. They ordered salame, olives, cheese, white braided bread, and two bottles of red wine.

"See," said Signor Ditto, "we eat here just the same things we have at home. I don't see why you could not all have come to my house."

"Oh, Ditto," said his wife. "It's so nice to eat out once in a while. Isn't it, Allinda? Don't you sometimes get tired of cooking?"

Julio and Nino sat alongside each other at one side of the table. The goat lay under the bench and the dog at their feet.

"I don't see why they don't have something more fancy to eat at fairs," said Julio, disappointed at the plain food being served.

"They are serving something fancy. See over on that table," said Grandfather.

The two boys looked and then shouted, "Gelati! Oh, may we have some gelati?"

"Of course," said Grandfather. "Of course."

He motioned to the waiter.

"Two double-sized ice creams," he said.

"It's a grand fair so far," said Grandfather. "I sold twenty gallons of olive oil and five sacks of corn to a merchant from Viareggio. He paid me in advance, too. There's a trusting fellow for you!"

The old man opened a leather bag and took out a handful of coins. He gave Allinda a gold coin and each of the boys small silver pieces.

"A lira apiece. You'll spoil them," said Signor Ditto. "Why, a lira! I never saw one until I was twenty. You are spoiling the boys, Padrone. Be careful. Money is hard to earn. It doesn't grow on trees," he said, shaking his head and winking at Grandfather.

"Twenty cents," said Nino. "I wonder what I can buy." He held the coin and turned it over and over.

"I know what I'm going to buy," said Julio, thanking Grandfather. "I'm going to——"

Just then the ice cream, colored red, white, and green, was set before the boys.

[165]

"Now, this certainly is something special," said Julio. "Look! Sugar spun to make a nest and three red cherries like eggs in it. It is something special, indeed! Santa Maria, save me from a stomach ache," said Julio, picking up the nest with the three cherries.

He put them in his mouth.

"The eggs taste much better than the nest," he said.

Signor Ditto looked at his son and said: "I think I'll walk back to the house and feed the pigs."

"Oh, forget the pigs, Ditto! Have some more wine. Waiter, more wine," said Grandfather. "Two large bottles."

Signor Ditto reproached Grandfather for buying wine. "Why buy wine," he said, "when just around the corner I have a cellar full!"

"Drink, Ditto, drink. You'll need strength if you want to throw the bear this afternoon. He looks pretty healthy to me, Ditto. It's going to be tough work. So drink up. It will make you feel stronger."

Signor Ditto looked askance at his wife and said: "I'm not afraid of the bear. Last year I was in poor health, but this year I'll show you."

"Ditto, stop bragging. You know I don't want you to take any chances with the bear. A man with your temper has no business playing with bears, especially a gypsy bear. You're no longer young, you know that," said Signora Ditto seriously.

"You're not afraid of the bear, are you, Father?" said Julio. "You can throw him, can't you?"

[166]

"Of course I can!" bellowed Signor Ditto, pounding the table with his fist. "Of course I can! Just you watch me."

Overhearing this part of the conversation, people began to look at Signor Ditto with interest.

"There," said Julio, "didn't I tell you my father wasn't afraid of the bear? You'll see. He'll throw him. You just keep your eye on my father when he gets in the ring with the bear, Nino. You just keep your eye on him. You'll see."

"Hush up, Julio. Your father is crazy if he thinks I'll let him go in the ring with that bear. Enough nonsense is enough," said the fat Signora aside to Allinda.

"I think the bear is tame, Signora Ditto," said Nino. "I can tell by the way he looks at people. He seems awfully gentle to me."

"Nino, you keep out of this," said Allinda. "If Signor Ditto wants to prove he can throw the bear, it's his affair."

"But, Mother, the gypsy bear is not as strong as last year. Signor Ditto is bigger and stronger than the bear."

"Another glass of wine, Ditto?" asked Grandfather.

Luncheon over, the group left the table and walked around the square, looking into the various booths. Julio passed the booth with the alarm clocks once more and looked longingly at the largest one. The square was filling again, more and more people coming into the village. They flocked from all the neighboring countryside. Men carried children on their shoulders so they could look over the heads of the crowds around the booths. The noise was much louder now. From the gypsy corner came shouting of "Bravo! Bravo!"

Allinda said: "Come, Maria, I have a gold coin. Come and help me spend it. I saw a booth filled with the finest laces from Venice. Let's go there first. Then we can make the round of the other booths."

Signora Ditto was an expert at judging laces. She could always tell whether or not they were good.

"That will be splendid, Allinda," she said, then pointing a warning finger at her husband she called to him: "Stay away from that bear!"

"You and Allinda go and look at the lace. I'll take care of myself," he said.

He was quite provoked.

Nino and Julio were the first to reach the gypsies. They forced their way between the spectators and stood in the front row along with the other children. Inside a circular enclosure, just high enough for the children to see over comfortably, the bear was dancing on his hind legs, holding a

[168]

pole in his paws. He tramped up and down, first on one foot then on the other. Sometimes he balanced his front paws on a huge ball. The gypsies were playing native tunes on a violin and a guitar. Some tapped tambourines in time to the melody. The bear danced to the music and the children clapped their hands and stamped their feet. A sharp whistle from the handsome gypsy brought both the music and the bear to a stop.

Nino said: "Now the gypsy will give a little speech like he did last year. Then he will wrestle the bear just to show everyone how easy it is to throw him. You'll see, Julio, how easily the gypsy will handle the bear."

The handsome gypsy picked up from the ring a tambourine full of pennies which the spectators had tossed into it. He counted them rapidly, and handed them to an old woman with a wrinkled face and white hair that hung over her eyes. She grinned and held the tambourine in her lap.

"*Signore e Signori, ascoltate*. Ladies and gentlemen, your attention," said the tall gypsy. "As you know, we go from village to village entertaining, mending pots, telling fortunes——"

Someone back in the crowd shouted: "Telling lies and stealing chickens!"

The gypsy hesitated for a moment, then went on: "—and we try to please everyone. Our work is good. Our entertainment is good. Further, events which we have forecast have come to pass for people of this and other villages. Our fortune telling is true. We, the gypsies, some of us of noble birth and others of humble parentage, do much good in——"

A voice back in the crowd shouted: "Vagabondo!" meaning vagabond.

The tall gypsy appeared a little offended, but went on with his speech.

Nino said: "There is sure to be stabbing if this keeps up."

"Oh, no, Nino. It isn't that bad. Wait. No one has called him a donkey yet."

"—going from village to village wishing good fortune to all. To you who are standing before me, we wish the greatest fortune of all."

Everyone clapped and shouted: "Bravo! Bravo! Now you wrestle the bear for us. We want to see if the bear is stronger than he was last year. Presto! Presto!" the crowd shouted. "Begin, begin!"

They waited impatiently while the brown bear sat looking mildly over the crowd.

Nino said: "There he goes. He's taken the pole away from the bear. Now we'll see."

The bear gave the tall gypsy a slap on the back with his paw as the man stood the pole upright at the edge of the ring.

Julio's goat was annoying some of the spectators in his effort to escape from the crowd. Signor Ditto stood by Grandfather on the opposite side of the ring. The gypsy informed the anxious spectators that the bear was getting stronger every year, but he would do his best.

"At the last village he threw me almost instantly."

The bear, knowing what was about to happen, started for the gypsy, caught him around the neck with his paws, and hugged him tight. The crowd yelled and the children screamed. Then the bear let go of the man, who fell to the ground, where the bear pounced on him. They tussled about for some time, the advantage changing frequently. First the bear would be underneath, his feet thrashing in the air, and then the gypsy, with his legs flying about like a windmill. Finally, the bear succeeded in throwing the gypsy on his back. The man struggled and made strenuous efforts to move the bear. Very slowly, he managed to lift the animal off, then turned him over and held him down. The bear didn't struggle. He just lay there, his shaggy head turned to one side.

"The bear is weaker this year. He is much weaker," Nino said to Julio.

"I hope my father wrestles him. He will be famous if he throws the bear."

"I think your father will have no trouble at all," replied Nino. "The bear doesn't look half as strong as he did last year. Did you see how easy it seemed for the gypsy to lift him off?"

Pennies stormed the ring. The gypsy bowed and smiled. Everybody shouted: "Che forza! What strength!"

"Who will wrestle the bear next?" asked the gypsy, motioning for the crowd to be quiet. In his hand he held another tambourine full of pennies and counted them over rapidly, before handing it over to the old woman.

Then he said to the crowd: "You have been generous with your pennies. There are exactly ten lire in the till. Now," he continued, "we, the gypsies, just to show our gratitude for your generosity, will make a prize of it. The whole ten lire will go to the man who throws the bear."

"Fair enough! Fair enough!" came shouts from the crowd. Some said he was a noble man.

"I'll wrestle your bear," came a husky voice from the rear.

Nino recognized it as the voice of the village blacksmith. Turning to Julio, he said: "Your father hasn't a chance now. He'll throw the bear in the twinkling of an eye."

Julio shouted across the ring to his father: "Hey, Father, I thought you said you could throw the bear? Why don't you go ahead?"

Julio's father was about to step into the ring, when the

heavy-set blacksmith, looking very grouchy, jumped in ahead of him. He took the bear by surprise and, catching him round the middle, lifted him right up and then let him fall to the ground. The bear sat stunned for a moment. Then he scrambled up and started after the blacksmith on all fours. The blacksmith hopped and dodged about, trying to keep out of the animal's way, but the bear caught him and in a very short time pushed him down. He held the struggling man with his back firmly pinned to the turf, while the crowd cheered loudly. They were not at all sorry for the blacksmith. They shouted with delight at his discomfiture and threw more and more pennies into the ring.

After watching the result of this match, Nino said to Julio: "Maybe the bear *is* stronger this year. He has just thrown the strongest man in the village."

"Oh, no, he hasn't," said Julio. "My father hasn't wrestled him yet. Father, Father!" shouted Julio across the ring. "Now is your chance! Go after him. See, the bear is sitting down now."

Julio was interrupted by the tall gypsy's voice.

"Well, well. We, the gypsies, still hold the prize. Who will wrestle the bear next?"

There was an expectant hush. No one said a word. Across the square the municipal band was softly playing a sentimental air.

Julio shouted: "Father, Father! Now is your chance to—" But before Julio even had time to finish, his father had jumped into the ring. He drew his belt up good and tight, spat on his hands, and stood facing the bear, who sat on the ground licking one of his paws through the heavy muzzle. All Signor Ditto's friends clapped their hands and shouted: "Bravo! Bravo!"

The bear still sat. Signor Ditto stood over him, going through all the motions of wrestling, hopping and skipping about the ring like a clown. The bear continued to sit and ignore the capering Ditto. The people in the crowd held their sides with laughter.

"Go after him!" they shouted. "Give him a kick! Make him get up!"

The tall gypsy standing at the edge of the ring shrugged his shoulders and shook his head at the bear's seeming lack of interest. Signor Ditto was still prancing about like a two-year-old colt. The crowd began to guffaw, first at the bear, then at the gypsies, and even at the puzzled Signor Ditto himself. They roared: "The bear is a fake!" They pointed at the gypsies, who seemed as much surprised at the bear's behavior as Signor Ditto.

Nino said: "There is something wrong, surely. Tell your father to get out of the ring before the crowd gets too angry."

"The bear is a coward. He knows my father is a strong man. He won't wrestle with him. He is a wise bear," said Julio. "He knows who he can throw and who he can't, all right. He's just a lazy coward."

At this the bear got up on all fours, just as if he understood what Julio had said, and began to circle around the ring huffing and puffing. Once he sneezed so loudly that the crowd surged backwards away from the barrier. Signor Ditto followed the bear around the ring with his arms out and his fingers clutching the air.

Julio turned to Nino and said enthusiastically: "Look at my father. If he had tights on, he would look like a champion. See him! Doesn't he know something about wrestling? Doesn't he?"

The huge bear, now tired of walking in circles, stopped and faced Signor Ditto, who waited in a crouching position for the animal to rise on his hind feet.

"Grr, grr, grr," the bear growled.

Signor Ditto started to reach for his handkerchief, but wiped his forehead with his hand instead. He made as if to jump out of the ring. The crowd, holding its breath, watched nervously.

Someone shouted: "Ditto, you get right out of there! Get away from that bear!"

The voice came from somewhere at the edge of the huge crowd. On hearing it, Signor Ditto made a leap for the bear, who, still on all fours, followed him around the ring with short sharp growls. He pushed the bear over and fell upon him with all his might. The crowd roared and shouted: "Bravo, Ditto! That's the way to do it. That's the way to do it."

Julio jumped up and down. "The bear is down," he said. "Hold him down!" he shouted to his father. "Hold him tight. See, see," he said to Nino. "Didn't I tell you?"

But by the time Julio could turn his head, the bear was

[175]

already sitting on Signor Ditto, who lay stomach down on the ground, working his arms like a swimmer in deep water. The bear sat on him and growled.

"Get up! Get up, Father!" shouted Julio. "Lift him off like the gypsy did. Up! Up!" called the wildly excited boy.

The crowd looked puzzled. So did Signor Ditto. Allinda and Signora Ditto, who had heard the shouts of "Bravo, Ditto!" pushed their way through the dense crowd and now stood beside Nino and Julio. Grandfather, with a smile on his face, stood on the opposite side of the ring. This smile hadn't changed since Signor Ditto leaped into the ring.

Signora Ditto crossed herself as she caught sight of her husband lying on the ground with the bear on top of him.

"Ditto, you fool! You fool, I warned you! Get out of there this minute!" she said, stamping her foot.

Allinda, thoroughly alarmed, stood beside her.

"Get up. Get up or I'll come in there myself."

She turned to the tall gypsy and screamed at him: "You tell your bear to let my husband up, do you hear me?"

The gypsy stood with arms folded across his chest and smiled faintly. He looked toward the fat Signora out of the corners of his eyes, then toward the crowd, shrugging his broad shoulders as if to say: "What can I do? You tell the bear!"

Signor Ditto struggled and squirmed with all his might to free himself, but the bear just continued to sit, occasionally giving the man below him a gentle pat on the sole of his shoe. Signor Ditto, now very red in the face, had made

[176]

several attempts at lifting the bear off his back and now lay angrily biting his knuckles. Suddenly he mustered all the strength he could and slowly, ever so slowly, he lifted the bear up, up, up. The bear fell over to one side and then with the speed of lightning was up on his hind legs. There was a rumbling of "oh's" and "ah's" and an occasional weak "He did it. Bravo, Ditto. Viva, Ditto."

Signora Ditto yelled for her husband to escape while he still had a chance. Nino stood with hands clutched tight by his sides.

Julio shouted: "Don't let him get you down again, Father!"

The goat had fallen asleep at Julio's feet. The band had abandoned the stand. Its members trooped now toward the gypsies' corner like an army on parade, and everyone, including the Mayor, his wife, and the priest, stood fascinated, looking on at the fight. The "Viva, Dittos" had died down and the crowd was again silent. All at once there was a commotion at the ringside. The excitement and suspense had proved too much for Signora Ditto, and she had fainted. She lay on the ground, her face very pale. Murmurs of apprehension came from the crowd.

The bear took advantage of this distraction. In the twinkling of an eye, he tripped Signor Ditto to the ground, and was sitting on him once more. This time, however, he sat on his stomach. The Signor lay with his back to the ground.

"The bear has won the contest," said Nino in a sad sort of way.

[177]

He saw tears in Julio's eyes and he wiped them off with his hand.

The gypsy, seeing that the crowd had become more and more angry, stepped into the ring and, holding a string of three sausages high up above his head, spoke to the bear in a jargon foreign to the peasants. The bear sniffed, turning his nose up to the sausages, and then down to Signor Ditto. Finally he decided that he preferred the sausages and lifted his head to the gypsy, who took the muzzle off him. One by one the bear ate the sausages. He squatted close to Signor Ditto, who was sitting up with a shamefaced air. A few people in the crowd laughed at first. Soon they were joined by others, and before long the entire gathering was roaring with laughter.

Julio and his mother, who had recovered from her fainting-spell in time to see the bear eating sausages instead of her beloved husband, stood in the ring beside the limp and bewildered wrestler of bears. He sat rubbing his eyes and lacing his shoes. Grandfather, Nino, and Allinda, standing beside Father Bellarosa, discussed the entire performance with smiles on their faces. The gypsy walked to the middle of the ring.

He glanced about and, seeing that the ring was bare of pennies, said: "Ladies and gentlemen. We, the gypsies, still hold the prize. Will anyone else wrestle the bear?"

Picking out the huskies of the village he pointed at them in turn. "You, will you?"

The peasants one by one left the ringside. They shook

[178]

their heads, gesticulated to one another, and made their way toward the booths.

"I am so sorry, Signor. I am extremely sorry," said the gypsy as he brushed the dirt from Signor Ditto's shirt.

The grinning, white-haired old gypsy woman came up to the group, holding a copper pot full of pennies.

"Would you care to have your fortune told?" she asked, cocking her head a little to one side and looking up into Signor Ditto's dazed face.

She grinned, but it was a gentle grin this time.

"No. I don't want my fortune told. I know enough about myself already," said Signor Ditto, and he walked away in a huff, supported by his son and the fat Signora.

Grandfather, Nino, and his mother followed close behind. The gypsy gave the bear three more sausages and then put on his muzzle. The handsome gypsy looked toward the parting group and smiled. Nino thought it was the most beautiful smile he had ever seen on the face of any man.

The Dittos started home, Julio still leading his goat by the rope. Nino, his mother, and Grandfather strolled about the square from booth to booth. Nino was looking for something he would like to buy as a present for his mother and Grandfather with the twenty cents he held tightly in his hand.

The sun threw long shadows over the square. They crept up slowly, shadowing the white campanile and the façade of the church. The medley of colors became subdued and gray. The Dittos had not returned. Nino knew that with the setting of the sun the Fair would be almost over, so holding his coin tightly he went from booth to booth looking for something on which to spend it. He stopped before one strewn with Venetian laces.

"Can I buy this for ten cents?" he said, holding a delicately laced handkerchief of pure linen in his hand.

"They are two for that price, my dear. Are they for your sweetheart?" asked the old lady in charge.

"They are for my mother. I'll take two."

Pipes and snuff boxes decked the next booth. Nino saw a beautifully engraved metal box, which he bought for his grandfather. On making his way toward Allinda and Grandfather he passed the booth where he had first met Julio.

Julio's goat stood tied to the booth. The man was winding up an alarm clock for a customer, but Nino noticed that the largest clock in the booth was gone.

The alarm clock the man was holding went off with a loud buzz. Startled by the noise, Nino looked back as he walked away. He saw Julio's goat tugging sadly at the rope.

That night after supper Allinda, Grandfather, and Nino went back to the Fair. The square was ablaze with the lights of lanterns hung on poles over each booth. The gypsies sat in a circle around a blazing fire of fagots and logs, singing and playing on stringed instruments. A young gypsy girl, dark-eyed and dressed in a full skirt of red and yellow, danced vivaciously, whirling her slim body to the tune of the gypsy

music. One hand was on her hip, the other lifted to hold a tambourine which she shook rapidly with quick jerks of her wrist. Around and around the fire she whirled, the red and yellow of her dress blending with the firelight. The huge brown bear lay sprawled on the ground fast asleep behind the gypsy musicians. Nino saw the handsome gypsy take a violin out of a velvet bag and carefully pluck its strings. He ran the palm of his hand up and down the bow, and then, waiting for the proper moment, he joined in the music. The tones of his violin—loud, deep, and plaintive—filled the night air. Nino, listening, imagined he could hear the voices of gypsies who had lived long ago crying out in the music of the violin.

Allinda, feeling the boy's hand trembling as she held it in

hers, looked down to see tears in his eyes. Nino hung his head as Allinda wiped the tears away.

"It's the violin, Mother. It always makes me cry," he said.

"It is something more than the violin, Nino. The music of the gypsies gets into everyone's soul. Freedom and the everlasting wandering of the gypsy race have made their music unlike any other."

"Have they always wandered about, Mother? Have they no village of their own? No place or home?"

"No, Nino. The gypsies do not live in villages, and their home is the open road. They never stay long enough in any place to call it their home. It's been that way with the gypsies for ever so long. They cherish their freedom and love to wander about the world in search of some new adventure. Here today, gone tomorrow," said Allinda.

The gypsy music was interrupted by a loud blare from the village band. The contrast between the stringed instruments and the horns was appalling. The combination filled the square with discord, and until the gypsies gave up their playing, it was impossible to distinguish between the two. The crowd threw pennies to the gypsies and then wandered off.

The dim golden light from the lanterns hung over the heads of the people and bats flew overhead. A crescent moon, pale yellow and with its points upwards, rocked in an indigo sky. The gray tower beside the church loomed huge and dark, piercing the heaven, which was sprinkled with twinkling stars.

[183]

Above the din of the crowd and the blare of the village band, Nino heard threatening shouts. They came from the booth where he had last seen Julio's goat tied. It was the booth with the alarm clocks.

"Mother, I think I hear Signor Ditto's voice," said Nino.

"Let's go over and see," said Allinda to Grandfather. "Perhaps Signor Ditto is angry about Julio's trading the goat for that clock."

They made their way towards a dense crowd of peasants who stood silently listening to a dispute between Signor Ditto and the owner of the booth. Julio and his mother stood behind Signor Ditto. Signor Ditto, with sleeves rolled up to his elbows, was shaking a fist at the clocks-seller.

"You sharper!" yelled Signor Ditto. "I have a mind to bite off your ears! What do you mean by taking advantage of my boy like that? A big, full-grown man like you trading one of your worthless clocks for a real live goat, and with a little boy too! You ought to be ashamed of yourself. I have a mind to call the police," said the angry Ditto.

The goat, still tied to the booth, maaed loud and the crowd roared. The owner of the booth stood behind the counter with folded arms, unmoved by Signor Ditto's threats and his brandished fist. Overhearing the disturbance, two officers made their way through the crowd.

"What's wrong here?" they asked. "What's the trouble, Signor Ditto?"

Signor Ditto, red in the face, began to stammer. "This sharper, this infidel, has cheated my son. See that fine goat

[184]

there?" he said to the officer, pointing. "It's my son's goat. Do you think it is a fair trade?" he appealed. "Do you call it a fair trade? I ask you."

Nino recognized the officer who had given Julio and himself a ride on the merry-go-round that same afternoon. The officer stroked his mustache and smiled.

"Oh, Signor Ditto," he said. "A bargain is a bargain, all the same. You had better give up now. The dancing will start soon and I'm sure you and Signora Ditto will want to dance."

He patted the angry Ditto softly on the shoulder.

"Come away. We don't want any trouble."

Signor Ditto still insisted. "My son has been cheated out of a good goat, and I don't think it is fair. I want the man to give my boy his goat."

The man behind the booth became impatient and said: "Look here, Signor, you are making a scene. It will do my business much harm. If I give you back the goat, will you be satisfied? Will you go away?"

"Certainly I will go away. First give me the goat. Julio, where's the alarm clock?" he said. "Julio, where are you?"

But both Julio and Nino had disappeared during the interruption caused by the officers. They were nowhere to be seen. Signor Ditto scratched his chin and stood helplessly facing the man with the goat. Allinda and Grandfather made their way through the crowd in search of Julio. The fat Signora followed, walking carefully so that she might not tear her new dress in the crowd.

[185]

She muttered as she went: "Oh, that boy, that boy is breaking my heart!"

They went from booth to booth searching, asking, but Julio and Nino were nowhere to be seen. Signor Ditto joined the others. He was angrier than ever.

"If I could only get hold of that boy, I'd make him remember this Fair for a long time to come!"

"Have patience, Signor Ditto. Boys are boys, you know; be calm. They are here somewhere. Let's look over under the tent. Maybe they have gone to trade the clock for ice cream," said Grandfather, laughing.

"That boy would trade his shirt for something to eat, and I still can't make out why he traded the goat for the clock," said Signor Ditto. "Queer boy, my Julio, always up to some strange mischief."

"He is just like you were when you were a boy, Ditto," said Signora Ditto to her husband. "You were anything but an angel, and every time I think of what a fool you made of yourself this afternoon, I feel embarrassed for you. Between your wrestling the bear and trying to start a quarrel with the clock man, I'm all worn out."

As they walked toward the tent, the crowd started dancing. The band was playing a lively piece and the young men and women whirled about happily. The four entered the tent and found a game of lotto in session. A group of villagers sat around a table covered with cheeses, salami, baskets of nuts, chickens and ducks, and various other things tradable at the Fair. Julio's alarm clock stood in the middle

[186]

of the heap and Nino sat beside Julio, who, with a flat card before him, listened intently as each number was called out by a man standing at one end of the table. Each of the participants had a card resembling Julio's with numbers printed on it. The man called out: "Number ten."

"Oh, Nino, I've got it!"

The man called another number.

"Twenty-one!" he shouted.

"You haven't that number, Julio."

The man just across the table was running a score fairly even with Julio's. There was a matter of only a few numbers between them. Julio trembled as each new number was called.

"If I lose the clock, I may as well run away from home. My father will be so angry, I'll never hear the end of it."

He looked toward the man calling the numbers.

"Eight, seventeen," came the numbers one after the other. Julio's card was almost filled.

"Oh, oh," he stammered to Nino. "I've got to win!"

"You will," said Nino, looking around the table.

The other players were not taking the game with the same seriousness as the two boys were.

Julio looked up to see who had put a hand on his shoulder. On seeing his father, he almost collapsed.

"Julio is winning!" shouted Nino. "See, Signor Ditto. After Julio saw there was no use in trying to get the goat back, he decided to try his luck at something else."

Signor Ditto, seeing the table heaped with food and the

[187]

almost filled card of his son, gazed around at the cards of the others. Yes, Julio was way ahead of anyone else. This served to subdue his anger, and he stood watching the game. One by one the numbers were called until only three remained. Julio had only one space left to fill on his card and the man across from him had two.

"Number five. Only two more to go!" rang out the voice of the man as he held up the small round wooden counter with a number five on it.

"You've done it!" shouted Signor Ditto. "You've won, Julio! Your card is filled and you have the highest numbered card in the lot."

"Hurray, hurray!" came the shouts of the crowd. They were glad that Julio had won, and each forfeited whatever he had placed on the table.

"Winner takes all!" shouted the man, pointing to Julio, whose first movement was to reach out for the clock.

Handing it to his father, he said: "I'm awfully sorry, Father. I'm so sorry to have caused you so much trouble. Now we can give back the clock, and everything will be fair all around."

"Oh, no, Julio," said Signor Ditto, shaking his head. "A bargain is a bargain. Remember that the next time you trade anything with anyone. A bargain is a bargain. Don't you ever forget that."

CHAPTER X

CHRISTMAS

"GOOD MORNING, Mr. Rooster," said Nino. "A pleasant morning to you."

The little colored rooster stood on the shelf above Nino's bed and didn't make a sound.

"You crazy rooster! The least you could do is to flap your wings and give a crow for me," said Nino. "On this, of all mornings, you should crow."

He laughed and, looking up at the rooster, went on talking. "You silly rooster. You just sit and sit. You never do anything else, unless someone blows the whistle under your tail. Even then you don't crow so loudly, but I love you just the same."

[189]

Nino still lay in his bed, nestled under the warm woolen blankets. He heard "crunch, crunch" noises out in the courtyard.

"Mr. Rooster," he said, "someone is coming to our house."

He sprang out of the bed, rushed to the window, and threw open the sash. Newly made footprints showed in the white snow. They reached across the courtyard.

"I wonder who it can be. Look!" he said to himself. "There are tracks to the hen house, the pig sty, and tracks from the entrance, too!"

The snow lay white and crystal-like below. The cold air began to chill Nino's face and he shut the window. He peered through the windowpane a moment, then went down the stone stairs in leaps.

"Good morning, Mother," he said. "Good morning, Grandfather. Who came to the house this morning? I saw tracks in the snow leading up from the gate."

"Those are Grandfather's. He fed the stock," said Allinda. Seeing Nino still in his nightshirt, she cried: "Nino! Nino! What in the name of all the saints do you mean? Go right back upstairs this minute and get into your clothes. Do you want to catch a cold?"

"No," answered Nino and went flying up the stairs, his nightshirt waving as he went.

He dressed hurriedly and twice found that he had put his smock on inside out.

He said with a voice full of glee: "Mr. Rooster, this is

[190]

the day before Christmas. Don't you know? Don't you understand? Why don't you crow? Why don't you crow? All right," he said, "don't crow, then!"

And again he went sailing down the stairs.

"Polenta, polenta, and covered with cheese and honey too!"

He ran to the table and sat down beside Grandfather.

"Isn't it grand out? Isn't the snow beautiful?" he said.

"Don't get so excited," said Allinda. "It will upset your breakfast."

"Are we going to the midnight mass tonight?" he asked. "Are we, Grandfather?"

"We will if we are not snowed in by night," said the old man, pouring coffee in a red terra-cotta cup.

He drank the black coffee steaming hot. Nino didn't see how he could do it.

The day was a long one for Nino. He watched his Grandfather carving patterns on a strong willow branch which was to make a small cane. He cut the bark, leaving a dark green and white pattern along the length of the cane.

"May I do the staining, Grandfather?" he asked.

"All right, son. Get the colored inks."

Nino, sitting on a stool, dipped the brush into the bottles. Rings of bright yellow, zigzag lines in red, animals and diamonds in blue stood out after Nino applied the colors to the wood.

"This one is for Julio, isn't it, Grandfather?" said Nino.

"Yes, it is," the old man replied.

The soft snow fell all day long, drifting this way and that. The grape vine hung like a mass of twisted white crystal on the arbor. The oven looked like a huge white ball. The bells rang many times during the morning. So muffled were their tones that Nino thought they sounded as if they were wrapped in woolen blankets.

That evening a quietness, still and mysterious, hung over the village. Nino, dressed in heavy woolen trousers, with a foxskin cap pulled down over his ears, stood waiting for his mother, who was tying a huge knot in a heavy, red woolen shawl. It covered her head and hung down on the sides, covering half her body. They were going to midnight mass. It was dark. Nino, his mother, and Grandfather made their way through the snow. The falling snow kept piling up on Nino's foxskin cap.

"Look, Mother! It's up to my knees already. By morning it will be up to my chin," he said, laughing.

Once he fell going through a heavy drift, and almost disappeared from sight.

"How warm the snow is!" he thought to himself, lying there for just a moment before he scrambled up.

It was fun going to church at midnight. They passed dimly lighted windows. Nino could see oil lamps keeping watch over the Virgin Marys that stood on recessed window-sills in houses along the way down the hill.

The church was dimly lighted. Long chains of evergreens went winding up the pillars on each side. Sprays of greenery covered the altar, and the oil lamp that hung over it had been covered with translucent paper. It hung like a huge five-pointed star.

Nino said: "Jacobo is playing unusually well tonight. Do you hear how softly the music comes from the organ, Mother?"

A little manger stood in front of the altar beneath the huge star. Nino could see the golden yellow straw around the infant Jesus.

After mass was over, a procession of peasants in single file started up the aisle toward the manger. Each in turn kissed the feet of the infant child, who with outstretched hands gazed up into the faces of the peasants. After each kiss, the priest blessed and wiped the tiny feet. Peasant after peasant stopped and kissed and then made the sign of the cross. The long procession moved slowly. At last it was Nino's turn to kiss the tiny feet. They felt cold to his lips. He noticed that some of the paint was worn off the tiny toes of the child Christ and wondered how many times they had been kissed before. The procession ended, a final prayer was said, and the people streamed out of the church and went home. On his way home, Nino could still feel the cold, tiny feet of the infant Christ on his lips.

Nino was awakened next morning by the sound of a Christmas carol. He sat up in bed.

"Chimes!" he cried.

He rubbed his eyes, looked about the room. The music came from under his bed. He sprang out and picked up a music box. A note fastened to it read: "From Julio to Nino."

[193]

"Oh, thank you, Julio," said Nino to himself. "It plays grand music."

The box played "Noel, Noel." On a chair stood a box of paints and under it some paper and brushes. This was from his mother. A package covered with bright green paper stood on the chest of drawers. Nino saw the inscription, in a floriated hand, which read: "From Jacobo to Nino."

"Oh, Mr. Rooster, isn't Christmas wonderful?"

Allinda and Grandfather came into the room. They both smiled and said: "What is all this fuss about?"

"Look, look!" cried Nino, pointing about the room and jumping up and down with joy.

He unfastened the cord around the green box and pulled out a flat round package all wrapped neatly with thin white paper.

"Oh, a della Robbia bambino!" he said almost breathlessly as he unwrapped it and set it gently upon the chest.

"It is beautiful," he said.

On the round plaque was an infant with outstretched arms and swaddled in cloth, white and tan, against a pale blue background. A wreath of pomegranates, apricots, cherries, and apples mingled with flowers of many colors encircled the little figure. Nino set the music box before the plaque. "Noel, Noel," sounded the tinkling chimes, filling the room with good cheer.

They went downstairs. A fire was crackling under the black kettle. On the mantelshelf stood a jumping jack done in bright colors. This was Grandfather's gift to Nino. Also,

there was a box of candy from the pastrycook, a hen with a flock of chicks from the priest, all carved in wood, and last of all a book from the Dittos. It was the story of Pinocchio.

Nino read several pages.

"It reminds me of Julio," he said.

For the rest of the morning Nino was lost in the pages of *Pinocchio*. Noon came. The family had been invited to the Dittos' for Christmas dinner. As they went down the hill and through the village, they were greeted with "*Buon Natale*" from everyone they met.

On holidays such as Christmas Jacobo the artist, who was unmarried, was showered with invitations for dinner. He had a hearty appetite and relished good cooking. Knowing what

Christmas dinner at the Dittos' held in store, he had refused an invitation to dine at the Mayor's house.

Signor Ditto had shoveled his small courtyard almost clean of the snow, which he dumped into the street.

"Let the Mayor worry about it," he told Grandfather as they entered the courtyard.

Signor Ditto looked tired and his face was flushed. Nino thought he seemed to stagger a little. Julio, who came out to greet Nino, was wearing a pair of leather boots that came up to his hips.

"How do you like my boots?" he said. "Father bought them plenty large enough. He said I would grow into them."

"They look fine and strong," answered Nino, looking the boots over. "But I'm sure they're a little large for you."

"Oh, well. What's the difference?" said Julio with a shrug. "What's the difference anyway? I'm growing so fast, I'll soon outgrow them.

"What did you get for Christmas, Nino?" he asked.

"Julio, I want to thank you for the music box. It was nice of you to give it to me."

"Oh, think nothing of it," Julio replied airily. "Think nothing of it!"

"Guess what the priest sent me, Julio."

"I can't guess," said Julio. "You tell me."

"He sent me a hen with baby chicks all carved in wood. Wasn't that nice? Now the rooster has a family all his own."

"He sent me a whip," said Julio. "A colored one. I can't understand Father Bellarosa sending me a whip."

[196]

Signor Ditto leaned on his shovel, talking with Grandfather and Jacobo in the courtyard.

Allinda, who had been listening to their conversation for a few minutes, finally shook herself and, saying: "Brr," she hurried into the house out of the cold air.

The sky was crystal clear. Nino saw the shadows beneath the leafless trees.

"Look, Julio! The sun makes blue shadows under the trees."

The donkey cart stood in a shed with its shafts pointing upwards. Grunts and squeals sounded from the pig pen and the clucking of lazy hens could be heard coming from the stone coop at one side of the yard. The goats went about rubbing their noses in the snow. Gray smoke from the huge chimney rose almost in a straight line into the sky. The satisfying smell of rich sauces was wafted from a window near the chimney and Nino sniffed the air hungrily while Julio looked in the window.

"Am I going to be hungry today?" he said to Nino. "Am I hungry right now? Hurry up, Mother. Hurry up the dinner, will you? Do you want me to starve to death?" said Julio, sticking his head through the open window.

A zoccolo flew over his head, barely missing it. Nino picked up the wooden slipper. The front part was covered with embroidered velvet. It was Signora Ditto's slipper.

"Once she hit me right on the head," Julio said, and taking off his cap he continued: "I still carry the scar. See? Feel there." And he ruffled his long curly hair.

Nino searched and found a little white patch on Julio's head, without any hair growing on it.

"Oh," he said. "Did it hurt much?"

Julio went into such terrific exaggerations that at last Nino said: "Let's go in. It's cold out here."

"*Buon Natale*," said the fat Signora Ditto to Nino as she limped about with only one slipper on.

She took the slipper and shook it at her son.

"He insults even his mother. And on Christmas Day, too!"

She stood with arms akimbo, still holding the slipper in one hand.

"No wonder the good priest gave you a whip for Christmas. He should have sent it to your father instead, who gives you altogether too much rope!"

Signor Ditto was warming wine. On each side of the fire a row of bottles glistened.

"Maria, Maria, calm yourself. Have patience with the boy on this holy day," he said kindly.

The Signora told Allinda that Julio took after his father. Both father and son were hot-headed. She said a little prayer to herself in atonement for having temporarily lost her temper on Christmas Day, and went to stir the risotto. On a table near the fire were two pans heaped with grouse and wild pheasants, all ready for roasting. From the oven beside the fire came the smell of baked rolls. In a recess beside the oven, fagots and wood were piled to the ceiling. Dried peppers, onions, and garlic hung in strings from the rafters. Nino

[198]

always felt at home in the Dittos' house, because it was so like his own in many ways.

Julio took Nino upstairs to see his Christmas gifts.

"See," said Julio. "There's the whip. And your mother gave me this," he said, holding out an image of the Virgin in colored plaster. "The bambino looks a little like you, Nino," he said, smiling.

It really did resemble Nino.

"This makes four Virgin Marys we have in the house now," continued Julio. Holding an ocarina to his lips, he played "Noel, Noel," and then, stopping for a minute, said: "I like this best of all. Thank you, Nino. Thanks a lot for giving it to me. I do hope I never break it."

Julio then showed Nino the colored cane which both Nino and his grandfather had worked on the previous day.

"What did your mother and father give you, Julio?"

"The boots are from my father! This is from my mother," he said, showing a Holy Bible. "It has a picture on almost every page."

"Julio, I will show you the box of paints my mother gave me. They are beautiful! And the good Jacobo, he sent me a porcelain della Robbia bambino all in colors, too."

"Like the one in the church baptistry with a wreath of fruit?" asked Julio.

"Yes, like that, only much, much smaller," said Nino.

They walked to the window. The vineyard outside lay covered in snow. The gnarled vines stretched out in long rows, bare and brown. Snow birds flew among them.

Patches of white with blue and purple shadows lay on the hills above the vineyard and blended into the rich dark green undergrowth. A thread of sparkling diamonds wound its way down the hills through a little valley.

"It is the brook sparkling in the sun. It is singing 'Noel, Noel,' too," said Nino to Julio.

Downstairs, Signor Ditto was saying: "Maria, why don't you put on the embroidered tablecloth? You know the one I mean."

The fat Maria said: "I was thinking of using it today."

In her youth Signora Ditto had gone to a convent school in Milan. It was there she had been taught the art of needlework.

The huge cloth lay on the table.

Jacobo said: "Signora, it is beautiful!"

The two boys hurried down the stairs and found Jacobo carefully examining the fine stitches and intricate patterns of the cloth. He was highly excited both by its beauty of pattern and by the excellence of its execution and said: "Signora Ditto, you should have stayed at the convent. This is a magnificent piece of art."

The Signora blushed at this compliment and replied: "Oh, Signor Jacobo, you flatter my needlework."

The pheasants roasting on the spit sputtered and sizzled. Allinda with a wooden spoon kept watch over the risotto, which had to be stirred often so that it would not stick to the pan. The room was filled with the spirit of Christmas. Neighbors who came to wish the Dittos a Merry Christmas

were heartily greeted by the Signor, and none left without drinking a glass of Ditto's wine. And with each successive caller Signor Ditto poured a fresh glass for himself.

Just as the church bells were ringing the noon hour, the Dittos and their friends sat down to the table all ready for the Christmas dinner.

Each person said the "Our Father" and then Signor Ditto proposed a toast to the group as he held a glass high: "May your health be heavy and your worries be light."

Nino thought it a strange sentiment for Christmas time, but, then, Signor Ditto was a strange man.

Everyone lifted his glass to the house of Ditto. Nino and Julio drank the toast in watered wine. A huge bowl of steaming risotto which had been set in the middle of the table was passed round, with grated cheese to sprinkle over, and the diners made short work of it. Next came the grouse and pheasants, roasted to a savory, shining brown.

Signor Ditto, from his end of the long table, kept saying: "Have more of this" and: "Have more of that."

His own plate was filled with the carcass and bones of a grouse.

"You must eat when you come to my house. Here, Nino, take this," he said, sticking a fork into half of a roasted pheasant and putting it on Nino's plate. "You don't want to go home hungry, do you? Look at Julio. Already he has finished a whole pheasant, while you have eaten only your risotto."

Nino finally did justice to the bird before him. At the same time he wondered where Julio put all the food he ate.

"In Florence," Signor Jacobo told them, "it is a crime to hunt and kill or snare pheasants; there is a law forbidding the hunting of other fowls, too. You may do this only in stated seasons, and even then you must have a permit."

"I'm glad I don't live in Florence," said Julio.

"My brother in Florence doesn't have to hunt. He raises pheasants for the table. He raises them like chickens," said Signor Ditto proudly.

"I don't mind anyone eating pheasant and grouse," said the fat Signora to Allinda, "but the tiny sparrows, I do feel sorry for them."

She shook her head sadly while holding a drumstick gently in her hand.

A huge platter of mixed vegetables and chicken came next,

swimming in oil and garlic and with a heavy, rich, red sauce over it.

"Doesn't that smell good?" Signor Ditto said to his guests seated around the table.

"What is it?" asked Nino. "It certainly does smell good. Is it more pheasant?"

"That," said Signor Ditto, "is *pollo alla cacciatore*, chicken in hunters' style. I made it myself."

"Did he, Signora Ditto?" asked Nino. "Did he really make it? Did you cook it too, Signor?" he said. "Your father is a good cook, Julio. It tastes grand."

His plate was heaped so high that Nino felt sorry he had been quite so enthusiastic over the Signor's cooking.

"When you finish that, I'll give you more," Signor Ditto promised.

Nino replied: "Thanks, but this will last me for some time to come." And as he gulped down the stew, he wondered how much more he would have to eat.

The large plate stood in front of Julio.

"One, two, three," he counted as he picked about in the stew and then looked round at everyone else's plate. "How many chickens did you put in the stew, Father?" he asked.

"Four," said Signor Ditto. "It takes four to make a good stew."

"Well, then where's the other gizzard? I can't find it," said Julio, looking at his father. "You know I like the gizzard best of all. I don't care so much for drum sticks, but I do love the gizzards."

[203]

Everyone laughed and his mother said: "Julio, don't be such a pig. Maybe someone else likes gizzards besides you."

Julio held one up on his fork, saying: "Would anybody like a gizzard? I've got three," with the hopes that everyone would say: "No." But to his amazement they all cried: "Yes, yes, yes!" Julio was much taken aback at this unexpected answer, but he found out that they were only teasing him. Down went the three gizzards, one after another. Nino suspected that Signor Ditto had already eaten the fourth himself.

The salad came next. Sliced onions and cold codfish that had been put in vinegar and olive oil overnight lay sliced between thick, pickled red peppers, and the smell of garlic predominated above all else in the bowl.

Nino had to say: "No, thank you," to Signor Ditto as this dish was offered him.

Julio took most of the cold codfish, but left the onions and peppers for the others.

"It's too bad Christmas doesn't come every day," he observed.

Signora Ditto answered: "Shame, Julio. How could Christmas come every day? A child like our 'Gesù' is not born every day. That would be too much of a good thing."

Jacobo, who up till now had been busy eating, said: "It might be a good thing, Maria."

Nino enjoyed the sweet macaroons. He wished that they had been served at the beginning of the meal instead of the end. The candied chestnuts were delicious, too. His mother had some in jars at home but they were not yet ready to eat.

It was the middle of the afternoon before they got up from the table. Outside, the sky had darkened, and snow was falling. Nino went to the window and, putting his hand out, caught some of the tiny flakes. They melted quickly on his warm palm.

Jacobo sat by the fire and played soft haunting music on his violin. Allinda and Signora cleared the dishes from the table, washed them, and then put them in a rack by the fire to dry. Grandfather smoked his pipe and Signor Ditto sipped his after-dinner liqueur.

Presently Jacobo laid down his violin carefully and said: "I shall be most happy if you will all come to my shop. We will roast chestnuts and have coffee around the fire."

Everybody accepted Jacobo's invitation. Nino clapped his hands with joy.

"Oh, that's a perfect way to end Christmas Day!" he said, going to fetch his foxskin cap and heavy sheepskin coat.

A visit to Jacobo's shop was always a source of inspiration to Nino. There was nearly always a new drawing or a new statue to be seen.

Nino and Julio rushed out. It was very cold and the snow was falling softly. The goats were huddled in the shed under the donkey cart and the pig pen was silent. They made their way towards the artist's house, which was not far from the Dittos'. It was near the church, directly across from the public washing place. Julio's big boots kicked up the snow with each step that he took.

"Look, Nino. There's ice in the wash pond," he said, pointing to the large square pool where the village women washed their linen. All along the stone edge of the pool icicles hung like sparkling white glass. A muffled sound of water came from above the pool. They passed a few villagers bundled up in shawls and heavy coats. White steam came from their mouths. Nino's nose got redder with each step he took.

Jacobo unlatched the heavy door and they entered. The big studio was lighted with tall candles, and a fire blazed at one end of the room. There was a faint smell of cooking, incense, and moldy clay. A large oaken chest stood in a corner heaped with tubes of paint and brushes and disordered piles of paper on a large board. Big calipers, modeling tools, and mallets were laid at random on a long table. An immense easel holding an unfinished Madonna in red chalk stood directly beneath a skylight. The artist's apprentice Alberto, who was deaf and dumb, was seated by the fireplace. He greeted them humbly; opening and closing his mouth, he went through the action of speaking, but did not utter a sound. He moved his hands rapidly at Jacobo.

"Alberto wishes you all a *Buon Natale*," Jacobo said.

Signora Ditto, shaking hands with him, said: "I'm glad to see you, Alberto."

Alberto nodded his head and smiled. He understood what people said, for he could read their lips. Chairs were brought up for the group. A huge crucifix, made of black walnut and with a figure of the Lord on it beautifully carved out of white pear wood, hung over the mantel. The well-modeled body

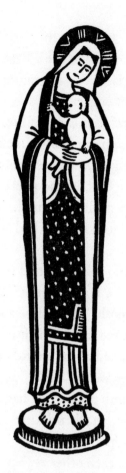

of the Saviour had been polished with beeswax till it shone in
the candlelight. Two richly colored round stained-glass
windows were on each side of the cross. High along the
whitewashed walls and near the colored ceiling hung fourteen panels done in tempera. The figures on these panels,
heavily shaded in rich browns, reds, blues, and greens, with
here and there a touch of bright jewel-like color, stood out in

relief. They were the stations of the cross. Jacobo had painted them when he first moved to the village from Florence. On the rear wall hung a large curtain, hiding the work on which Jacobo was at present engaged.

It must be wonderful to live in a home like this, thought Nino as he looked from one beautiful object to another. He hoped that he too might become a great artist like Jacobo.

He lifted the linen curtain and peeked behind it.

"Oh, oh!" he said softly to himself. "Oh, my!"

He quickly turned to Julio, who had already stuck his head in all the way.

"It's an organ," said Julio in a loud voice.

"Sh! Be quiet, Julio. It's a surprise," said Nino, holding a hand over Julio's mouth. "It must be a surprise for us all, or Jacobo would not have covered it up."

The two boys walked away towards the fireplace, saying to each other as they went: "Sh!"

The deaf and dumb apprentice had brought the coffee, and now sat on the hearth pricking chestnuts. Nino and Julio went to help him.

"Sh!" they said to each other as they helped Alberto with the nuts, smiling at their discovery, which was a secret between them.

It did not take long for the nuts to roast. The group sat around the fire nibbling chestnuts and drinking black coffee. The sound of the evening bells from the church came faintly through the falling snow outside into the brightly lit studio. Everyone made the sign of the cross hurriedly and then con-

[208]

tinued to nibble and drink. Alberto brought more coffee, which he poured into each cup. He then threw another log on the fire and sat down on the edge of the hearth. Sitting there, he busied himself in peeling chestnuts, which he put into a glass jar.

Jacobo said: "Alberto prefers his chestnuts cold, the day after."

One day the artist had found his apprentice eating watermelon all by himself. He was eating the rind first. Alberto always left the best part for the last. It was that way with many things that Alberto undertook.

Jacobo told stories of artists who had lived long ago. He told how Michelangelo, while at dinner with a group of artists, painted a fly so naturally on his plate that all his companions believed it to be alive. Jacobo told the group around the fire that Michelangelo was so great that once he was asked to submit plans for a new cathedral. The Pope summoned all the artists who had taken part in the competition before him with their plans.

"Michelangelo went, too," said Jacobo. "Mind you, though," he said, smiling, "he had no elaborate plans or drawings with him. He appeared with his hands in his pockets."

Nino listened intently, his mouth wide open.

"What did he show the Pope?" he asked Jacobo.

"Oh, Nino, he brought his own genius with him," said Jacobo, "the greatest thing that he possessed."

"What's that?" said Julio. "What's genius?"

[209]

Signor Ditto said: "Wait, Jacobo will tell you soon. Listen to the story now."

Everyone was deeply interested in Jacobo's story of the great master. Alberto sat on the hearth and twiddled his thumbs. He had been present at the telling of this story many times before.

"Well, Michelangelo brought his own genius. . . . Go ahead, Signor Jacobo," said Signor Ditto.

"Well," continued Jacobo, "Michelangelo stood with his hands in his pockets.

"The Pope, who was in ill health and consequently irritable most of the time, said: 'Well, friends, unroll your plans and let me see which of you has designed the best cathedral for me.'

"The anxious artists unrolled their plans and drawings. On seeing the drawings before him, the Pope became more irritated than ever.

"He pounded his fist on the table and bellowed: 'Dolts and blockheads, do you call these cathedrals? Are you artists? They're no better than plans for hen coops and pig pens.'

"The artists withdrew, hanging their heads. The Pope then called Michelangelo to him.

" 'And you, my good man, what have you brought?' "

"Now we'll find out," said Julio to Nino.

"Sh!" said Nino. "Sh!"

Nino was trembling.

"Well," said Jacobo, "Michelangelo went up to the Pope. He knelt, kissed his hand, and said: 'Your Holiness, I humbly beg your pardon. My time has been so taken up with trying to finish the Sistine Chapel that I have been unable to make any plans or drawings for the new cathedral.'

"The Pope coughed and smiled. He knew the ability that Michelangelo possessed.

" 'Well, what do you intend to do?' said the Pope.

"Michelangelo bowed his head a moment.

" 'Well, come, come, my good man,' said the Pope.

" 'I intend to prove to you that with the proper time I can design the best cathedral,' he said to the Pope.

" 'And how can you do that?' asked the Pope.

" 'Bring me a large sheet of paper,' said the artist.

"They brought a very large sheet of paper. Everybody present, including the Pope, was amazed at what Michelangelo did. With a crayon and with one continuous sweep he had drawn free hand a circle so perfect in form that when a compass was placed over it, it proved to be without the slightest fault.

" 'Michelangelo,' said the Pope, 'come here, give me your right hand.'

"The Pope kissed and then blessed it and said: 'You and you alone shall design the new cathedral.' "

The group was spellbound by the story Jacobo had told them. Alberto had fallen asleep by the fire and was gently snoring away. Jacobo shook him lightly and the boy leaped to his feet and placed another log on the fire, which had burned low.

"A great, great genius was Michelangelo. You should see

[211]

the Sistine Chapel. It is eternal!" said the artist excitedly. "It is magnificent!"

Later Julio asked Nino if he knew what the word "genius" meant.

"You know, the thing Michelangelo brought to the Pope in place of plans and drawings," he said to Nino.

"Oh, that," said Nino. "Jacobo told me. It's something that every great artist is born with. It's a gift from God. It's something inside you. I can't explain it to you, Julio. But, anyway, Jacobo said in order to be a great artist you must have it."

Jacobo displayed a new model in wet clay.

"It is just merely roughed in at this point," he said. "It is a new Virgin Mary for a church in Lucca."

It looked complete to Nino. The artist covered it up with a wet cloth.

"It keeps the clay moist and easier to work with. Come some day, Nino, and try your hand at modeling. I will show you how to build the armature first."

"Oh, do you really mean that?" said Nino.

He couldn't wait to get his hands on the clay.

Jacobo took a deep interest in the boy. "He has talent, lots of talent," he told Allinda one day, after she had shown him the drawing of the procession.

Grandfather stood in the middle of the room, staring at the curtain.

"Is it a secret?" he asked, winking an eye at Jacobo.

"No, it's a surprise," replied the artist, beaming all over.

[2 1 2]

"It must be a big one, Jacobo," said Grandfather, surveying the huge curtain.

Nino said: "Sh!" to Julio.

Allinda said: "A surprise!"

The fat Signora repeated: "A surprise?"

"I'll bet it's another big painting," Signor Ditto said.

"No, you're wrong, Father. It's, it's an——"

Nino called out: "Please, Julio, hush up!"

Jacobo motioned the two boys to come to him. He bent down and whispered something to each boy and said to the others: "Wait."

The three disappeared under the huge linen curtain. Allinda and Grandfather and the Dittos waited. Alberto stood with his arms crossed and watched. He knew what was behind the curtain. The wheezing sound of bellows was heard by the people in the room. Allinda heard Nino and Julio giggling and the voice of Jacobo saying: "Quiet, boys. Quiet now."

The suspense was becoming unbearable, when at last a peal as of thunder broke the silence, followed by deep melodious tones that melted from one chord into another. Allinda, Grandfather, and the Dittos sat as if petrified. A rich melody rose in waves to the vaulted ceiling of the studio, fading at last into silence.

Jacobo came out from behind the curtain, beaming from head to foot, and said: "It's the new organ for the church! I finished it this morning. The last part came from Florence three days ago."

[213]

He threw aside the curtains.

"Look!" he said. "Isn't it magnificent?"

Nino and Julio had followed Jacobo out and stood before the huge organ.

"Think of it," said Nino to Julio. "Signor Jacobo made it all by himself, too."

"It's much better than the old organ in the church. It sounds louder, much louder too," said Julio.

"Look at the beautiful carving on it," said Allinda to her father. "See the little cherubs carved on the tall reeds. They have their mouths open as if singing."

"That's where the music comes out, Mother," said Nino. "And, Mother, isn't it wonderful the way Jacobo has carved the two angels on each side? They look as if they are holding the reeds up straight. Signor Jacobo, it's the most magnificent organ I have ever seen! Will you play it for us again?"

"Someone will have to work the bellows for me. No wind, no music," he said, laughing.

"Nino and I will pull the levers," said Julio, who found more pleasure in pumping the organ than he did in the music.

Jacobo seated himself at the organ.

He turned and said: "If you will all sit at the other end of the room, it will sound much better."

Grandfather, Allinda, the Dittos, and Alberto (who couldn't hear a thing), all sat by the fire. Jacobo played the organ as they had never heard him play before. He started with soft lingering bass tones, and gently blended them with

[214]

minor and major chords, intermingled with sacred trembling
chimes. With bent head the artist swayed, then paused,

touching first this stop, then that, changing the tone. He played on and on, one piece following another.

"It's like a church," thought Nino.

"Jacobo lives in a church," he said, looking about him, and for the first time he understood why Jacobo was such a pious man.

His violin, his paintings of saints, his love of music and all things beautiful made for this strong feeling of devotion in the man. Nino felt a little awed as he pulled the lever up and down. Jacobo was playing a lively air now, not so sad as those before. It made Nino feel better.

Finally he stopped altogether and said: "Thank you, Nino, and thank you, Julio, for pumping the organ."

Allinda, Grandfather, and Signor Ditto complimented Jacobo on his fine performance. The Signora was smiling and wiping her eyes.

She said: "Jacobo, how do you do it?"

"Someone is knocking on the door," said Julio. "Maybe it's the police. Maybe the organ plays too loudly," he said to his father.

Jacobo opened the door and exclaimed joyfully: "Come in, Father Bellarosa! Come in. You are just in time for black coffee. Did you hear the organ? It's finished, and the tone is just as I wanted it to be."

The priest stood in the doorway.

"Did I hear the organ?" he said. "Look, look, Jacobo," said the good priest, pointing out the door. "They heard it too."

[216]

The snow fell on a throng of peasants standing in the
street before Jacobo's shop. They huddled close together as if

to keep themselves warm from the night's chill. They looked eagerly toward the open door and the priest.

Voices shouted: "*Ancora! Ancora! Musica, musica!*"

"They want more music," said the priest.

"I can't have them all in here," said Jacobo. "The place isn't large enough."

He peered at the crowd.

"No, Father, I couldn't get them all in, but I'll play for them though."

Jacobo left the door open and seating himself at the organ played once more. This time it was the Christmas song "Adeste Fideles" ("Come, All Ye Faithful"), and soon the peasants outside caught the strain and one by one they knelt in the snow. They sang the strain over twice. Then the priest said that after that they would have to come to church to hear Jacobo play on the organ.

"It is the new organ to take the place of the old one," he told them.

The crowd dispersed and one by one went back to their houses.

Signor Ditto shook hands with the priest and said: "Oh, Father Bellarosa, it is a magnificent organ!"

"Did you all have a good Christmas?" asked the kind priest of everyone in the room.

"We have had a glorious Christmas, haven't we?" said Grandfather, speaking for the group.

"And Jacobo with his music has made it perfect," said Nino, feeling the effects of the night's celebration.

[218]

Signor Ditto offered to help move the organ to the church piece by piece with his donkey cart.

Alberto gazed at the organ with a look of sadness on his face. Allinda was getting ready to depart. Nino thanked the priest for the carved hen and the baby chicks, thanked Jacobo once more for the della Robbia bambino, and they left. Julio had fallen asleep, and his father carried him home in his arms.

Grandfather, Allinda, and Nino walked up the hill to Casa Checchi, and Nino thought he heard strains of music in the falling snow.

"Noel, Noel," it seemed to whisper to him in the silent night.

CHAPTER XI

A NEW YEAR'S GIFT

For five days snow had fallen on the hillside and the village. It drifted down lightly from an ashen gray sky, forming a vast white blanket over the land. Never before had the villagers seen so much snow. It had been snowing since Christmas, since the night that Nino had gone to Jacobo's house. Allinda, Grandfather, and Nino peered out of the windows of Casa Checchi and looked down upon the village, which lay shrouded in a thick blanket of snow. The marshes in the distance were only faintly discernible through the falling flakes, and the leafless trees in the olive grove below them looked like ghosts with their gnarled white-covered branches. The dome of the church was like a huge white snowball set on the top of the building. There was little to do but to wait until God willed the snow to stop falling. In the meantime neighbors struggled waist-deep through the drifts to see one another. The livestock snug in their stalls and pens were fed every day from the winter storehouse.

Unable to go outdoors, Nino spent much of his time drawing from memory. He mixed numerous color combinations from his new box of paints, trying to get as many tints from one color as he possibly could. The cupboard in Casa Checchi was filled with food and there was little to worry about. Grandfather said he had seen it snow for five days before.

"It nearly reached the eaves," he said to Allinda and Nino at supper, while they were discussing the present fall.

As the evening approached and it grew darker, Nino watched the blinking lights in the houses down in the village. The falling snow made them look like the stars in the Milky Way. Nino, standing by the window facing the courtyard, wiped the pane now and then so as to see out more clearly. The deep-set edge of the window was piled high with snow, and he could hardly see over the white flakes heaped high against the glass. Allinda, who was working at the loom weaving a long strip of toweling, was silent and intent on her work. Now and then she stopped the motion of the loom to cut a knot near her, or to tie a thread that had snapped. She would knot it carefully and then look towards Grandfather, who was pacing the floor back and forth with one hand in his pocket, the other holding his huge pipe, from which issued great puffs of smoke.

Now and then he would absent-mindedly say: "If it doesn't stop soon, if it doesn't stop snowing soon, well, what will we do with all this infernal snow? It will swamp the lowlands. That's what it will do, as it did the time it snowed for five days."

[221]

"Cheer up, Father," said Allinda. "It will stop soon. Sit down and don't worry over the elements. God wills what He wills. There is nothing we can do about it and, besides, haven't we had a wonderful year? Good crops, everything in abundance. The cellar is full and so is the storehouse. It will be over soon, you'll see," she said and, rising from the stool at the loom, she threw more wood on the fire and lit another candle before the Virgin Mary in the place of the one that had burned away.

"Mother, Mother! Grandfather! Someone is coming through the courtyard!" shouted Nino. "No, it's not Signor Ditto! I can't make out who it is. It's too dark outside."

Nino, his mother, and Grandfather peered through the window. A short, stocky figure struggled through the snow, using his arms to aid his progress much like a swimmer. At each step he disappeared almost from sight in the deep drifts. They could hear the man talking to himself as he drew nearer to the house.

"It's the postman!" cried Nino. "It's Signor Barrilli, the postman, Mother. Perhaps he has come for help."

The short, stocky middle-aged man, his red face half buried in a heavy sheepskin coat, reached the threshold. Grandfather, recognizing him, flung the door open. The little man stamped his heavy leather boots and walked to the fire.

"What a lot of snow! Heaps of it, isn't there, Padrone? If it keeps up, we will need no post office, I'm sure," said the little man as he whirled his arms around and around to take the numbness out of them.

"Well, what brings you away up here, Signor Barrilli?" asked Grandfather. "You must be nearly frozen in this deep snow. How did you ever manage to dig your way up here?" continued Grandfather, helping the postman to remove his heavy sheepskin coat.

"It's not so bad, only in places," said the postman, blowing on his fingers.

"Since I haven't seen a letter from America come to this village for some time, I thought I'd better bring it up to you. It might be important news." Then he added: "There is a package, too."

"A letter for us!" cried Allinda excitedly. "A letter from America! Nino, Nino! It must be a letter from your father. Oh, give it to me quickly, Signor Barrilli!"

The postman reached deep down under his woolen shirt.

"It's here somewhere," he said, feeling about his waistline.

Everyone waited, and finally the postman pulled out an envelope.

"Yes, yes, Grandfather, it's—Nino, it's a letter from your father!"

Allinda held the envelope close to her bosom.

"Mother, please read it," said Nino, clapping his hands with delight. "Grandfather, you won't have to tell me a story tonight. Mother will read the letter. May I see the stamp, Mother? Is it the one with the picture of Lincoln, or is it the bright red one with the picture of Washington?"

It was the blue one with the picture of Lincoln. Nino had saved quite a few. Grandfather called them the great men of America.

"You know, Nino," he would say, "they are like our own great men, Julius Caesar, Garibaldi, and our good King Umberto."

Nino held the envelope for a while and thought of America. Often he had peeked into the mail box in the post office with the hopes of getting a glimpse of that far-off land. He handed the envelope back to his mother.

The postman made himself comfortable in a chair beside Grandfather, who had brought out a decanter of wine, some raisin and nut bread, and a small basket of chestnuts.

[224]

"You'll stay for a while, won't you?" he asked the postman, who looked as he would be quite content to spend the night at Casa Checchi. Nino sat near Allinda by the fire. She carefully tore open the envelope and took out the letter. Two yellow petals which had been dried and pressed fell to the floor as Allinda opened the folds of the letter. Nino picked them up and held them to the light of the fire.

"They are from a strange flower, Mother."

He held the petals up for Grandfather and the postman to see.

"They are from the poppy flowers that grow in abundance in California, Nino," said Grandfather. "Some day when you go there you will see these flowers covering the hills and making them a golden yellow in the sunlight. Allinda, please let us hear the news from America."

Everyone sat quietly while Allinda read out loud the news from Nino's father in America. Presently she paused, her eyes wide with astonishment at the surprising message which the letter contained.

"I am sending you money, my dear Allinda, enough money for a passage for you and Nino to this country."

"Oh, Grandfather! Oh, Nino! We are going to America. Think of it, Nino! You will see your father for the first time in eight years."

"Mother, Mother, read more, read more!" cried Nino. "What a wonderful time we are all going to have, aren't we, Grandfather?"

"Yes, Nino, what a grand time! It will be wonderful! It

[225]

will be splendid! Magnificent!" Grandfather said in a hoarse deep voice that seemed to carry a broken heart along with it.

The letter was by no means good news for the old man. Many a time he had felt sad at the idea of parting with Allinda and Nino, but had always consoled himself with the thought that, if the time ever came when such a parting might take place, he would prevent it somehow, no matter what happened, by finding a way to accompany them. As Allinda read on, plans for the future swam through Grandfather's distracted head and tormented him.

"I'll sell the land. Yes, that's what I'll do. I'll sell everything and go to America, too. What would life be for me living alone here without Allinda and Nino!"

His face brightened as this solution rushed through his head.

"I'll sell everything," he thought over and over again hurriedly, and he said aloud: "Oh, what a grand surprise, and coming on the last day of the year too! How wonderful, Nino! Now, now you will travel and see many things. You'll like America. It's a wonderful place!"

Allinda had stopped reading, to share her father's outburst of happiness. Nino was a little concerned about Grandfather. He had noticed the change in the old man's face as his mother read the words "enough money for a passage for you and Nino." His father had said nothing about Grandfather. Nino could not for a moment bear the thought of leaving him, of going away without him.

"We shall miss you," said the postman, pouring himself

another drink. "Well, here's to a bon voyage and good fortune in America. I wish I were going. I've never been there."

"When are we going, Mother?" said Nino. "Will it be real soon? Does the letter say?"

Allinda finished reading the letter.

"Soon, Nino, soon," she said, and looking at Grandfather she blinked her eyes.

Nino could see that his mother's eyes were moist with tears, though a faint smile still remained like a pale, pale flower at the corners of her mouth.

"Allinda, Allinda, come now! This is no time for weeping. It's a time for rejoicing. Think of it. It has been eight long years since you and Nino have seen him. Oh, it's time to rejoice! Come, come, soon the old year will go out and to-morrow will be the beginning of a new one. It will bring us all many, many beautiful things. Be joyous now, Allinda. Shame, my big girl weeping over good news!" said Grandfather, tenderly pinching his daughter's red cheeks.

"Surely, Mother, Grandfather is right. The old year goes and the new one comes. He is right, Mother. Cheer up. With the new year, new thoughts and new things come; and didn't Father send us a splendid New Year's gift? You'll see, Mother, everything will turn out all right. Won't the Dittos be surprised, and Jacobo, and . . . ?"

Nino's heart sank as he repeated their names.

"Let's roast some chestnuts, Mother. I'll prick them. Grandfather, you'll have some, won't you, and you, Signor Barrilli, you'll stay, won't you? Oh, I wish the Dittos were here. We could make a New Year's party of it. Wouldn't that be lots of fun? I'll go and fetch them!" said Nino excitedly.

The postman roared with laughter at Nino's suggestion of going after the Dittos.

"The snow was up to my waist coming up the hill, Nino. It would just about reach up to your chin. I wouldn't try going out if I were you," he said.

"Nino's suggestion is a splendid one, Allinda. I'm sure the Dittos will be glad to hear the news and, besides, it's early. The night is young. I'll go and ask them to come up," said Grandfather, getting up from his big carved chair. But Signor Barrilli also rose and, putting both his hands on the old man's shoulders, said: "I'll go, Signor Checchi. I'm much younger than you. I'll bring them back. Besides, being without wife or children—I love a New Year's party."

And putting on his heavy sheepskin coat, the little man disappeared hurriedly out of the door before Grandfather had time to protest.

Now that the entire course of her life was so suddenly changed by the arrival of the letter, Allinda felt a deepening affection for her friends, and the thought of spending this evening with the Dittos cheered her.

Nino, using a small knife, pricked the chestnuts one by one. He was rapt in deep concentration and his head was filled with scattered thoughts of the future. Things happen too quickly, he thought. A letter, words from another world, snow falling outside (in how many parts of the world was the snow falling this minute?) —his active little mind was alive and quivering with wild imagination. Thoughts raced through his brain, and the hot fire beating on his face filled him with emotion. One by one he put the chestnuts into the pan.

Grandfather sat in his big oaken armchair and watched Nino by the fire. This chair was three hundred years old and creaked and squeaked with every move of the old man's body. He was smoking his favorite pipe, a gift from his father. The bowl of the huge pipe had carved on it the face of a winking satyr with a mischievous smile.

Allinda read the letter over twice. She sat in a corner by the fire and, looking up, gazed thoughtfully a moment into the sparkling blaze. She got up and put the letter away into a carved chest near the loom. Now and then Nino rushed to the window to listen and to see if the Dittos were coming. He pressed his nose to the frosted pane until it became almost numb.

"Will the Dittos ever come?"

Outside, the tiny flakes fell slowly. They shone like a fine sprinkling of silver in the pale light cast from the window. Nino thought he heard Signor Ditto's voice singing out in the courtyard; rushing to the door, he opened it only to hear the muffled sounds of the church bells coming up from the village below. Grandfather and Allinda came to the door and stood beside Nino. They listened for a moment and then knelt in prayer to the sound of the evening angelus. The tiny flakes falling quietly found their way through the open door

[229]

and fell on Nino's face. The dark, silent evening was awakened by the sound of the bells, and the low voices of Nino, Allinda, and Grandfather joined together in prayer in answer to their tolling.

The prayer over, Nino said: "Brrr," and rushed to the fire. "I wish the Dittos would come soon."

He thought of the fat Signora Ditto, and with his eyes shut tightly he could see her bundled up like a ball, struggling through the snow; he could picture Julio on his father's shoulders. Nino's thoughts were interrupted suddenly by hearty shouts in the courtyard.

Laughter and the loud voice of Signor Ditto saying: "*Troppa neve.* Too much snow." Now and then at the top of his voice he sang: "*Vieni giù, vieni giù dal ciel.* Descend, oh, descend from heaven," and in a voice full of laughter he called to Saint Mark to stop the snow: "*O San Marco, basta con questa neve ora!* O Saint Mark, we have enough snow now!"

The group reached the door that had been thrown open. Stamping their feet amid cheerful greetings, they took off their heavy coats. The fat Signora was wearing three thick woolen shawls, one over another.

"Oh, Julio, we are going to America!" said Nino, helping Julio to pull off his heavy boots. "Oh, I wish you could come too! We would have lots of fun."

"Some day we are going to America, too," said Julio with a serious look on his face, "and then maybe we will see each other again. Maybe we will both be grown up by that time. Fancy us meeting, me wearing a mustache and you speaking a foreign language. Think of it, Nino. Why, when you get to America the boys won't understand what you say to them. You'll have to learn to speak all over again."

"My father said it's not hard to learn the language spoken in America. He knows lots of words already, and he never went to school there, either," said Nino. "Oh, the language will be a simple thing for me, Julio. It won't be so good not seeing you and all the others, but I'll send you lots and lots of postcards, Julio. Surely, I will," said Nino, getting up.

He looked his friend squarely in the face.

[231]

"I knew you would all come tonight. I've prepared enough chestnuts for all of us, and we will sit up to hear the midnight bells."

"I hope it stops snowing soon," said Julio. "My father says too much is entirely too much."

The group walked about the huge room all talking and babbling at once; confused questions filled the air.

"When will you start? By what way are you going? I don't like the sea," said the fat Signora. "I'm sure I'd get seasick. Oh, think of it, Allinda, you'll see the Statue of Liberty in New York. They say it is the biggest one in the world."

It seemed that Signor Ditto never went anywhere without first visiting his cellar, and out of his back pockets now came two long slim bottles. He was in good humor tonight.

"I'm glad the old year is almost gone. I get rather tired at the end of the year. It's like the end of a day. One always feels better at the beginning of a new day," he said, as he set the two bottles beside the stone walls of the fireplace in order to warm the wine.

The postman resumed his place in the chair beside the decanter and the friendly fire.

"It looks as though the snow will let up," he said. "I noticed that it was clearing a little outside as we came up. I wouldn't be surprised if New Year's Day were a bright one."

An exclamation of surprise from Allinda caused the group to rush to her. She had opened the package, which had been forgotten until now in the excitement caused by the news in the letter.

Holding up a stereoscope, she said: "I hope it has views of America." Allinda glanced quickly through the cards which accompanied it and said: "They are all views of America."

"What is a stereoscope?" asked Julio. "Is it something to eat?"

"Mother, may we look through the stereoscope? Both Julio and I want to see the pictures of America."

Allinda gave it to Nino, saying: "You and Julio take it first."

Soon the entire crowd sat around the candle-lit table and with enthusiasm peered through the lenses of the stereoscope.

"Oh, what a huge statue! It's the Statue of Liberty," said Nino; "and look at this one. It says at the bottom: 'Niagara Falls.' Isn't that a lot of water! I wonder where it all flows to."

The postman, looking at a snow scene in Central Park, said: "It snows in America, too. Look at the branches of the

[233]

trees. They're just covered with snow. It's all so real through the glass," he said, and handed the stereoscope to Grandfather.

The new gift was passed from one to another. It was a thrilling experience for them all. Yosemite Park, the Fair at Chicago, Old Faithful at Yellowstone National Park, the Brooklyn Bridge, and the Grand Canyon were viewed, each in turn. Signor Ditto looked at a picture showing a man in an automobile, and suddenly recognized the "horseless carriage." Finally the two boys were left alone with the stereoscope. Again and again they went through the cards. Nino's father had sent a set of twenty-four. Julio could not understand why the two pictures on the card turned into one when he put the stereoscope to his eyes.

Grandfather and Signor Ditto sat in a corner near the loom, talking in low tones.

Nino overheard his grandfather several times saying: "I'll just make it a short visit."

Signor Ditto said earnestly: "Oh, Padrone, don't sell. Don't leave the village for good. I'll see to it that everything is taken care of while you are away."

Nino's heart thumped heavily as he overheard this conversation between the two men. How good! he thought. Grandfather will be with us. The knowledge made him more cheerful. Leaving Julio alone with the stereoscope, Nino wandered closer to the loom, pretending that he was looking for something.

"Sure, Signor," said Grandfather. "I'll go, and I am in-

[234]

deed grateful to you for your goodness in taking care of Casa Checchi while I am away."

Nino walked nervously about the loom. He tenderly touched the woolen threads that were stretched taut on the frame, and with his ears wide open listened to the conversation.

"There's only the chickens and the pigs and goats," said Grandfather. "I will surely be back early in the spring to take care of the plowing and the planting, and, besides, I haven't been to America in forty years."

Nino stirred the ashes, moving the chestnuts and turning them over. Julio and the postman took turns looking through the stereoscope. It was quiet in the huge room while everyone waited for the chestnuts to cook. Allinda and Maria in the pantry were busy preparing olives for the midnight supper. Large black shiny olives were taken out of a small crock. They were heavily spiced with olive oil, cinnamon, and finely chopped garlic and parsley. Pickled onions, bright red bell peppers, and savory anchovies filled a platter; thin slices of salame stood heaped high around these delicacies. A large loaf of thick-crusted bread stood ready to be divided.

All this Allinda, with the help of Maria, placed on the table before the fire. The chestnuts had been heaped to one side and they stood in a neat pile along the stone wall of the fireplace, where they would keep hot. The New Year drew near. Voices could be heard in the night, voices coming from the neighbors down the hillside, sad voices lamenting the parting of the old year and cheerful loud voices praising the

[235]

coming of the New Year. Soon the church bells, tolling slowly at first, clanged out fast and joyously. It was midnight. The group around the fire at Casa Checchi stood up and drank a toast to the New Year and then they walked out into the courtyard knee-deep in snow, to breathe in the freshness of a new day. The snow had ceased falling and the dark quiet sky hung low over the surrounding hills. The moon turned to silver the slope where the monastery stood above Casa Checchi.

In friendliness the little group silently huddled together in the courtyard. Standing beside his mother, Nino felt a twinge of loneliness creep over him. This was the last time he would stand in the courtyard to greet the New Year. His thoughts wandered away through the night and to America. As he stood there in the courtyard with the others, listening to the clanging of the church bells and hearing the far-away cries of the villagers as they cheered the coming of another year, Nino wondered first where he would be and how he would feel on the next New Year's Eve. He glanced about the vast courtyard, bathed in a cold and silvery light. The half-moon seemed to rest in the arms of a tall mulberry tree, and the dark leafless limbs seemed to embrace the moon as if to say: "Stay awhile. Don't go away."

Nino watched the moon move over the tree. It moved ever so slowly up, up from one branch to another. In each branch the moon seemed to want to rest. Before Nino realized that everyone had gone back into the house, the moon had left the mulberry tree altogether. It soared high

up over the sky, lighting its way as it went. Nino's shadow
followed him as he walked towards the door of Casa Checchi. He heard his mother calling to him, and turned once

more to look up at the moon high above the mulberry tree and the monastery.

"You'll always follow me, won't you?" he said to the moon as he closed the door.

The group sitting around the table enjoyed the midnight supper. Everyone ate heartily. The blazing fire and the sputtering candles lit up the huge room. They were all in a cheerful mood.

"I feel better already," said Signor Ditto. "Oh, there's nothing like starting all over again. Now we are strong again. Salute to the New Year and to Nino, Allinda and"—he paused and winked at Grandfather—"and to the house of Checchi."

They drank the warm mulled wine.

The postman blinked his eyes and said: "What a blessing it is to have friends!"

Julio fell asleep on his mother's lap; clutched tightly in his hands was a large piece of cheese and bread. Chestnut shells littered the table and empty glasses stood as sentinels over the unfinished food.

Nino awoke early, long before the rising of the sun, and as he walked to the window he shivered. Grandfather was shoveling a path to the oven and Nino could see him piling the snow high up on either side along the path.

"Hello, Grandfather. Do you think it will snow any more?" cried Nino.

"Oh, hello, Nino. Why, you should still be asleep. You

went to bed so late last night, I'm surprised to see you up so early. Come down and give a hand. It will give you a good appetite for breakfast," said Grandfather.

Nino dressed and, putting on his boots and heavy sheepskin coat, clumped down the stone stairs. He was disappointed at finding his mother not up, and stole quietly into her room, where he found her buried under the covers. Kissing her gently, he went out into the courtyard. Grandfather handed him a shovel, and Nino worked in silence for a while.

Finally stopping his work, he said: "Grandfather, last night I overheard you and Signor Ditto speaking."

"Yes, Nino," replied the old man, "and what did you hear?"

"Are you really planning to go to America with Mother and me?" Nino asked as he looked up at Grandfather in a serious way.

"Yes, Nino. I have decided to go to America. We will have a grand time, won't we?" said the old man. "Why, we'll see everything, won't we, Nino?"

The two worked on in silence. The sun rose clear and penetrating over the brow of the hills.

"There is a thaw coming," said Grandfather. "Soon you will see the snow melt and the courtyard will look more like itself again."

"I'm so glad you will be going to America with us, Grandfather!" said Nino. "Oh, I'm so glad!"

Every day now Nino walked to the post office, and every

[239]

day no letter, no news, no passage. January passed. February came. Light cool winds blew over the village. The trees on the hillside showed signs of awakening and the slender limbs began to swell with the ripening of the sap. Life was starting anew. Spring was near at hand. At the end of February a letter arrived. It contained the passage money and directions. Preparations were made. A new trunk was bought and the house was cleaned from top to bottom.

Allinda and Nino walked about as if in a daze, looking intently at each object which they touched as if it were for the last time. The Dittos came to see them every day. Signor Ditto had scrubbed his donkey cart to a degree of cleanliness that might honor a prince. He was to take them as far as the station. The Signora wept every time she spoke to Allinda.

"Oh, Allinda, be sure and write to me," she said. "I want to know all about what you are doing while you are far away."

At last the day came when Nino, his mother, and Grandfather, surrounded by their baggage, sat in Signor Ditto's donkey cart. The cart looked like a moving van. Julio sat next to his father, who urged the lazy Bimbo on with gentle flips of the whip; if he didn't hurry, they might miss the train to Genoa. The heavily laden cart rattled through the village streets.

"*Buon viaggio!*" the villagers shouted after them.

Nino was filled with excitement as he glanced about at the stone walls of the houses and the shops.

When they reached Jacobo's house, he said: "I'd like so much to say good-by to Jacobo."

On hearing this, Signor Ditto brought the panting donkey to a halt. Nino sprang out of the cart and knocked on Jacobo's door. There was no reply. Disappointed, he climbed back into the cart. The donkey jogged along the road and drew up by a lonely railroad station at the edge of the marshes near Massa Carrara. The small stone building stood bleak

and bare in the morning sun. Only the long shining rails made it seem like a railroad station at all. Nino looked back towards the village of Massarosa. Never before had the village looked so far away to him. Even Casa Checchi seemed to be miles and miles up on the slope of the hills. Actually it was only three miles away. The golden yellow dome of the church shone brightly in the morning sun and the three crosses on the mount were hidden from view in the distance. Nino saw the steel railroad tracks winding through the marshes like long silvery threads. Suddenly he saw a group of people standing on the platform of the station. He walked towards them. He recognized Jacobo, Father Bellarosa, the pastrycook, the Mayor, and many others. A man came out of the building, set a flag in a hole in the platform, and then walked back into the station.

Jacobo was the first to approach Nino, handing him a small parcel.

He kissed him on the cheek and said: "God bless you, Nino. I'll miss you."

Father Bellarosa gave Nino a string of rosary beads and said: "Keep this always with you."

The pastrycook had a very large parcel, which he handed to Nino and said: "Wherever you go, you will never find sweets as sweet as these."

The March wind, the mild sun, and the crowd of people all seemed like a dream to Nino. Now the train was in sight; soon it drew up with a shrill whistle at the platform. Nino looked at the conductor in bewilderment. His was the first of many new faces that Nino would see.

Nino held in his arms a wicker basket and the parcel that Jacobo had given him. The rosary beads hung about his neck. Voices, voices, *addio, addio,* good-bys. Someone hugged him tightly. It was Signora Ditto. Signor Ditto was telling Grandfather for the sixth time not to worry about the stock. Julio took hold of the basket and helped Nino into the train. The throbbing of the engine mingled with the jumbled voices of the many friends gathered at the station to bid them farewell, making one confusion of noise, and above it all rose the loud hiss of escaping steam.

Much weeping and many *"buon viaggios"* filled the air as the train pulled out from the station and sped on through the marshes. Nino, his mother, and Grandfather gazed out over the lowlands and saw the corn and wheat fields flying by. Here and there the shimmering waters of the canal that wound through the marshes glistened in the sun. Massarosa lay far in the background, and Nino looked long at Casa Checchi as the train sped on. Clouds of smoke coming from the engine sometimes shut the landscape from view. The white smoke surged up and down before the window of the compartment. The clickety-clack of the rails became monotonous and worked its way into Nino's head. The landscape along the journey became more and more unfamiliar, and soon Nino was lost in new surroundings. The train stopped now and then along the steep cliffs of the Mediterranean, and as Nino looked down into the surging white and emerald green waters of the sea he felt dizzy.

On they sped through vast fields patched with newly turned greenish brown soil, past rolling hills with white stuccoed houses perched on them. Nino tried to count the telegraph poles, but finally gave up. Now they were speeding along the edge of the sea again. The sun hung over the water, and to Nino it seemed as though he had been on the train for years and years. The afternoon wore on, and at last he fell asleep.

"Nino, wake up!" cried Allinda. "Look, Nino! Did you ever see such a beautiful sunset? The sun is setting over the Mediterranean."

A long strip of land, dark blue in the distance, reached far out into the sea. It stood out sharply against the emerald green of the watery horizon and the coral sky.

"What a beautiful sunset, Mother!" said Nino, rubbing

[243]

his eyes as he looked out of the window. "It is the most beautiful one I have ever seen."

A solitary gray cloud edged with crimson followed the sun.

Allinda and Grandfather stood beside Nino watching the splendor of the parting day. Slowly the huge copper-colored sun sank into the water and disappeared from sight, leaving golden shafts of light that shot fanlike into the sky and became lost in the heavens.

Nino said:

"That's where America is—beyond the setting sun."